The Small Scroll: The Enlightenment of Jesus

ISBN

Paperback	978-1-68547-210-8
Hardcover	978-1-68547-211-5
eBook	978-1-68547-212-2

Library of Congress Control Number: 2023900705

Printed in the United States of America

wordHOUSE

101 Foundry Dr,
West Lafayette, IN, 47906, USA
www.wordhousebp.com
+1-800-646-8124

THE SMALL SCROLL

The Enlightenment *of* Jesus

CHRISTOPHER MILLER

Table of Contents

Author's Note

Before you begin to read this book, I would like to add a small note.

As this is a book about Jesus, most of us will have thoughts and questions rising up. Perhaps we are wondering how this book will compare to what we learned in Sunday school, or at our church, or to the writings of our own Christian Sect. We may remember when we were Born Again.

One thing Christians have in common is the bible. It is said the bible is the Word of God, putting it in a unique category. It is Absolute, and yet each and every one of our billions of people will have a different sum of understanding, a unique understanding of what we believe and what we do not believe.

As you read this book I ask you to avoid stopping and saying, "is that true, is that what I believe?" too many times. The book is like a river, it has a sound and flow that explains and expresses something more than the sequential words themselves. It will become evident in the same way a good detective novel grows more and more comfortable as you go along.

I really do hope you can find the sound, because this is the story and the story really happened.

-CM

Chapter One

There was a lot of fanfare around my birth. Of course, I don't remember any of that, but as I grew, I learned about it in small, almost shy increments. My mother felt she had to tell me, but I could see it was more out of a feeling of responsibility than enthusiasm. It was almost as if she didn't believe it herself, as if she had been told an important secret by a trusted friend or teacher, but still, on some level, she was unable to accept that what she'd been told was true.

I accepted what she did tell me in the same way. I was interested. I felt a certain excitement and a strong feeling of curiosity, but I sensed she didn't really want to talk about it, and as was my nature, I reacted to her nonverbal instruction and pretty much forgot aboutthe subject.

As I start this story, I want to talk to you about my humanity. I was a person, a human. I don't mean to say I was normal, but lifeseemed normal to me, and as I was growing up, I appeared normal to those around me. A child is special to its mother, and naturally, I felt that, but I had no sense of being different from other children.There is a lot of misunderstanding and controversy about my nature, but there is a lot of misunderstanding on this earth about everything. For those of you who believe I was the walking incarnation of God on earth, I ask you to read on a few more pages before you give up. You are not completely wrong.

Mankind has an intense desire to understand. The problem is that understanding is a big thing. Understanding itself cannot be truly represented or defined by a word—or a few words, or words at all—but we can talk about understanding, and even truth, in words, and that is good. That's what I am going to do as we go along, and hopefully, at the end, we will understand more. After my life as a man, a lot of words were written and spoken about me. Words like trinity and God were used, but really, those words do not help in understanding me or my life because they represent things so large and so beyond what any man can experience, understand, and then treat as simply a part of his vocabulary that to use them as simple definitions supposed to apply to me or the meaning of my life is somehow profane.

But to be a man is something we all understand to a greater or lesser degree, and that is what I was, a man. The only difference between me and the rest of the men on this earth is that I did not make the mistake that is measured in millionths of a measure. That is what separates me from the rest of mankind; I was perfect.

To use this first separation—perfection—in comparing me to the many worthy men who have lived would show only a barely discernible division between us, but the fact is that I made no error in my life. All other men do.

There have been, and are, great men who, if fairly judged by the tools available to mankind, would be equal in the majority of their lives to the majority of mine. But make no mistake; from the position of the Spirit of God, one side of the blade falls to life, and the otherfalls to death. No other subtlety exists.

One is true and alive; the other is gone in the oblivion of dust. Yet the lifetimes themselves could appear to human evaluation indistinguishable in virtue. So it was. I lived as any man, both loved and doubted. I lived the early part of my life hidden in normality, safe from the intensity of man's scrutiny and equally invisible to his ability to perceive me as something different, something important. It was this side of the equation that I later found most difficult. I enjoyed the anonymity of being human, but trying to show the truth of the other possibility, the possibility that I was different, perhaps imperceptibly but essentially, proved to be an illumination of how well the truth is guarded from the approach of man's understanding.

My first childhood memories were of Egypt. It was big, colorful,and, from my position on my mother's back, noisy, dusty, and wonderful. It was to Egypt that an angel had ordered Joseph to takemy mother and me shortly after my birth, saving me from death at the hands of a king fearful about the rumors that a savior of the Jewish people was soon to appear.

It was custom among my people to shelter the young, especially the firstborn boy, so whether in a small room hidden from crowded streets or on fur rugs and woven wool placed beside the fire, I grew up in a protected realm, the world of my mother. It was a world of serenity, beauty, and brilliant mornings; in the darkness of the early night, quiet flames brought contented drowsiness. They were days full of food, color, and women with laughing eyes, all busy about some duty that led from kiss to kiss and hug to hug.

I was young when my family, prompted by another angelic dream, decided to move back to Judea. I was three, or perhaps a little younger, when they first started packing. To me, the journey was pretty much a blur of carts, donkeys and bags with everyone moving in confused, crowded ways until the chaos settled to a slowly turning wheel of people, sky, and sand finally spilling out into the desert and the vast lonely confines of travel.

We never arrived at our intended destination, Judea. I remember talks between my mother and father late at night, when they assumed I was asleep. The talks rose and sank in intensity, with words and hidden lamps that I knew were unusual to the normal flow of night.

I supposed that during one of those talks, they decided to change direction, and we went to Nazareth, not Bethlehem. I later learned that Archelaus, the new king of Judea, was as virulently concerned about the religious rumors of a Jewish Messiah as was his father, Herod, making Judea dangerous for us.

Nazareth was a small, unnoticed city perched in the hills and valleys of Galilee. It was a beautiful place, perfect in the ways that only the memories of childhood can maintain. Since it was the village where my parents had lived before I was born, we settled into a home and a world that were familiar and easily accepted. My mother and father were less concerned with the rough physical environment than with the establishment of their hearth, a hearth protected and nurtured by the living light of the world's True Creator.

Nazareth looked over a gently curved valley extending into the haze of the distance, with much of the town sprawling into the shallow bowl of the valley and surrounded by the symmetry of hills that made the area so identifiable. It was a city—or a village, depending on who you were—small in comparison to the fortified cities of Japhia and Sepphoris, which were both nearby, but it was close to the trade routes, busy, and always up to date on the latest news of activities both political and religious.

We took up residence in a small house near the outskirts of the town, close enough for my father to buy his materials and attract some notice for his trade but away from the narrow, jostled streets of the market. By the time I was six, my father would take me to his workshop for a morning or an afternoon, and I'd sit quietly, watching. He even occasionally asked me to hand him a tool or a piece of wood. I loved the shop. I loved the smell of the different woods stored carefully above our heads in measured stacks to dry and await the moment they would be pulled out and fashioned by Joseph's skilled hands. I loved the golden light that filled the room as the warm sun found its way from one window to the other, touching the benches and the curious tools: clamps with threaded batons that tightened to the perfect grip and smooth-handled adzes made lustrous with use and the traces of finishing oils from my father's hands. The ocher walls held the light, still friendly long after the direct sunlight had left the room.

As I grew older, my cautious help became more and more frequent, until I received duties rather than requests, and the time spent with my father became routine instead of occasional. I think that was the happiest time of my life, although by age ten, my mind and eyes were often fastened on the hills and trees outside the window, and I was distracted by a quiet, fiery joy that waxed and waned between my heart and head.

The joy I felt came from spirit. The ability I had to feel that joy without question or insecurity came from the faith of my people and from my parents' comfortable dedication to that faith. By the time I was beginning to remember things, our religious life had settled down to routines that had been practiced by Israel since the time of Moses. That meant our life was based on the scriptures and the resulting knowledge of God. To upright and faithful Hebrews, which my parents and their parents had always been, God and the law were as real a part of daily life as the things of the earth. Food, air, love, anger, light, God, worship, study, worry, fatigue, and sleep were all simply part of their lives. If asked, a Hebrew would, of course, place God above all other things, but in fact, God was a fiber of the rope that made up existence, and that was that.

I loved this devotion and accepted it. I expected it just as I did our meals, and it was no coincidence that our meals were times when God and faith were inevitably as present as the food and utensils themselves. Each morning, my father would read from the scripture, and we would listen.

Sometimes my mother would ask a question or point out that my father could apply such wisdom to a particular task. She had a mischievous twinkle in her eye as she said it, and my father would smile to himself, shaking his head, and bring us back to the more serious nature of the text. When the reading and prayer were done, we carried on to the meal without pause, the contentment in our hearts a little stronger. Scripture, prayer, and food brought us back to the center after a morning or afternoon of worldly frustrations that would tire and confuse more often than not. Whether I was with my father in the shop, walking with him to the market, sitting with my mother at noon, or resting on her lap after the evening meal, God was never far away. Some little detail of life would always bring up a comparison to a proverb or a law: a lesson on patience, a gratitude for a beauty brought to notice, or a warning as to how hurrying caused pain or how the lack of attention caused a distress or sadness. Our recognition of a little mistake was a reason to be thankful to our Creator.

On the Sabbath, though, we truly focused on religion. When I was old enough, which wasn't very old, I had to struggle to read the scriptures themselves and remember the books, their order, and what the essential elements of each book or section were. I had to memorize certain scriptures according to a method and order passed down to my father as the recommended course of study, the one given to his father and his father's father. When my brothers and sisters came along, I watched as both my mother and father lovingly and with a kind of proud but serene elation repeated the lessons to each in turn. I also couldn't help but notice how they, especially my mother, sometimes smiled at some comment I made or stared at me as I repeated some verse or other. My mother often talked to me about the things she felt most closely, be they troubles, satisfactions, or questions about the deeper aspects of life. Some of this I knew was because I was the firstborn, but I also knew that some of it came from the things we rarely discussed; God had told my mother I was important to him and was in fact his Son and destined to rule over all of Israel.

When I noticed my mother staring into the far distance, I knew that in the hidden heart of mind and soul, she was remembering those times not so long ago when, as she had told me, an angel had spoken to her about my birth and life. Perhaps what most held her reverie was the fact she was a virgin on the day of my birth; my very existence was indisputable evidence of mystery.

I was, as were all Hebrew children, carefully nourished and educated in the truth by the community as a whole. We had the synagogue, the Sabbath, the festivals, and school.

The Sabbath was a thing unique to our people, but so was our God. To most tribes and nations of the world, gods were things that came along separately, products of folklore and myth, politics and nationalism. They created their gods with chisel and temple. The gods they imagined, formed, and shaped over time, became the gods that existed; gained and lost popularity; and faded with the fortunes of the nation. The exception is the children of Ishmael, who share the same God as the Jews, although their faith has realized a different destiny. This might seem a bit simplistic, but it is a point that reappears regardless of how deep you dig. To us, God was a thing outside our nation. He existed before and separate from us; in fact, He had chosen us, not we him, and to keep him, we had to live according to the law he had given us. The Sabbath exemplified this. This day was devoted entirely to worship and remembering the Creator of heaven and earth. It was a day when any kind of work or labor was forbidden; every moment was to be devoted to worship and thought, scripture and study, feasting and enjoyment. It was a cheerful day. It had a decorum, yes, but it was a time of celebration and love.

The synagogue was a slight departure from the law in the sense that strictly speaking, we were all supposed to worship at the temple in Jerusalem. The realities of the time made this virtually impossible, and within the newly fashioned traditions of the local scribes and Pharisees came the synagogue.

Despite a lack of formal acknowledgment from the priesthood in Jerusalem, by the time of my birth, every town or city in Israel had a synagogue. It was there the Pharisees and learned men gathered to worship, learn, and teach. It was there the men and women sat on the floor separately to recite the Shema, pray, read from the law and from the prophets, and hold discourse on what they'd read.

Although the synagogues had rulers, any worthy person could, and did, read and discuss the holy writings. On the morning after the families had answered the summons of the trumpet announcing the Sabbath and returned to their homes to feast, sing, pray, and enjoy their finest clothes, finest wine, and purest feelings, the community met at the synagogue to worship and celebrate the day devoted tothe Living God.

It was at the synagogue that I attended school. I didn't like having to leave my mother's side, and I missed the long mornings with my father in the workshop, where I was becoming, at least I thought, more and more useful. But there were lots of other children at school, and as I realized that a full understanding of the sacred writings was a larger task than I'd imagined and began to understand the methodical approach we would take to guarantee a thorough study, I started to get excited about the prospect of really learning about God.

Jews had little need for secular study. We had everything we thought was important to life within the context of our religion. We had language, poetry, geography, and even mathematics, and we had the transcendent joy of reaching understandings about ourselves and the world that reached the center of life. My young contemporaries and I began to feel the power of our God reaching into our hearts and minds, and soon everything we saw with our eyes was filtered through the mysterious light of a power more tangible and real to us than the signs of material power we were beginning to notice in the temporal world around us. At least I saw it that way, and I think the other boys did as well, in one way or another, but whereas the interest grew to boredom for some of my friends, my passion only increased with knowledge, and by the time I was twelve, I felt more than ready to accept the mantle of adulthood and embrace the full responsibility for my actions as judged by the God of Israel.

I had grown from a child to a young adult, and my understanding of the world reflected this change. It is not well known that a man reaches his intellectual peak in the year or two before the changes brought about by adolescence begin to rob him, hormonally, of the undivided use of his brain. Of course, in terms of knowledge and wisdom, like most men, I grew wiser and more knowledgeable as I grew older, but in terms of sheer energy and acuity, my mind was never better than in the years during which I was taken to the temple in Jerusalem to formally acknowledge my entrance into adulthood.

I had learned so much. I was full of enthusiasm and excitement. I had learned from the scriptures that the universe had an all intelligent Creator, a real person—not a physical person, of course, but a real person nonetheless. He was an aware, caring individual and a loving and powerful master of existence and was as wise as all wisdom and as kind and understanding as you would wish to be with yourself. I had learned how mankind had been cheated out of a joyful destiny, how the perfection of the world had been spoiled, and how the unity and freedom that should have blown through the earthly kingdom—through blossom and dew, morning and treetop, softness and beauty, and the simple dignity of the animals—had been lost. I knew that spirit-filled harmony should have transmuted the earnest thoughts of men into physical reality, the gift of worldly dominion given to man by a loving God. This gift of creativity should have allowed man to complete the patterns of life as intended, as had been woven throughout the eons of endless time. All this had been lost.

I had learned and thought about this, and then I had learned about it on a deeper level, even as a child. I had seen and felt moments when, even for the fortunate, the true gravity of our human plight broke through into that moment of physical, emotional, and intellectual awareness we called realization. I had felt shock and then the icy grip of nausea, which held my stomach for an instant as fear flashed through my body, leaving me cold and empty, alone with the terrible vision of the truth about humankind's desperate circumstance.

Even in Nazareth, this underlying discomfort was there—not obviously, but it was there. I had seen the flash of violence as a Roman soldier struck a lethal blow to a man who, just a moment before, had stood proud and critical, certain of his moral correctness, now irrevocably gone, torn and broken, a terrible opening to a nightmare just below the surface. I had seen the foulness of impending death as a ravished body was whisked away to some barren sanctuary outside the town walls. I had seen the eyes of women, men, and children so filled with despair and hopelessness that even death could seem a welcome friend. I had seen the filth of poverty and neglect; even by the age of eight or nine, I had seen enough to know that something was wrong.

But the brightness of my youth covered the lasting effects of such horrors, for I had also read the promises of scripture. I knew God would fix those things. In fact, I was more excited than worried about the prospects of what was to come, as much from the simple optimism of the young as from the uniqueness of my nature, and I pushed into my life, anxious to observe and be a part of the great event my community talked about and yearned for: the deliverance of my people. It was deliverance from Rome, yes, but more importantly, it was deliverance from the shackles of a dark and doomed world, from the unrelenting weight of a presence that, as much as it was ignored, always seemed to have the last word. It was deliverance brought about by the hand of God. It manifested as a feeling and a force that ran through virtually all of us in Galilee: anticipation.

So perhaps you can understand how happy I was when my parents told me they would be taking me to Jerusalem for the Passover. I knew the trip was not entirely for me—every family planned and saved to make the trip as often as they could—but I also knew it was no accident that my first trip to Jerusalem coincided with my coming of age. After the Passover at Jerusalem, I would be a man. I was proud about that, and I wanted to put my feelings of confidence and devotion to God to the test. There were things I had noticed that bothered me. Some were serious, such as the common and attractive rhetoric of the young men who talked about taking up the sword to free our people from the iron grip of Rome. Their arguments seemed convincing, and it seemed that scripture, to some extent, backed them up, for every Jew knew bondage was not our natural destiny, and I noticed that even the older men smiled and nodded approvingly when a passing orator would stir the crowds to passionate longing for action and the freedom it could bring. My parents did not share such views, and I was uncomfortable with them myself, but as a man, I could talk, think, and argue with the agitators and pacifists alike. I would decide, and the thought of finding out what was truly correct for me and for my people thrilled me, as much for the journey of learning as for the conclusions it would bring. Some of the things that puzzled me seemed less important than the issues of nationalism but, as it turned out, were more symptomatic of the web of error that held men so desperately captive. The pride of the congregation leaders, who seemed to miss the point sometimes but still managed to suffocate the enthusiasm of budding thought, confused me. They were often quick to dismiss the value of thoughts brought up by men of lessor public position, rejecting sincere ideas with disdain and citing platitudes often more fashionable than correct. I looked forward to my adult task of really learning the truth about those things, and the time was coming, although I, like all the young, didn't know then just how long it would be before I answered most of those questions.

Chapter Two

The party gathering for the journey was large. Traveling to Jerusalem was a serious and often dangerous undertaking, and it was advantageous to go in numbers. Consequently, many of the families from our surrounding areas had decided to band together. Most of the families knew each other or were related, and they had been planning for the event for months.

I could hardly contain my joy; everyone looked beautiful. The sky and sand were more vivid and sparkling than ever, and the power and feel of the coming spring seemed to shine out of the younger of us as if we simply couldn't hold it in. Even the older men, though busy with the animals and the stores and laden with the wonderful equipment of the full-grown man— leather and silver, metal and jangling loops, hidden sword and heavy water bags—couldn't contain their good humor, flashing smiles and bright commands to the boys who scurried around and whispering silent, mysterious messages to the women who flowed through the growing camp, effortlessly weaving the chaos into a caravan of color and purpose. It was good, and many friendly eyes met mine, sharing in an instant a wave of common understanding and shared happiness.

We took the directly southern route to Jerusalem, through Samaria. I didn't know exactly why. It was more common to circle east across the Jordan; the Samaritans were not known for their friendliness to Jews, but apparently, there was trouble on the more traveled path, and Roman soldiers— especially if they thought of us as connected in any way to remnants of recent uprisings— were more to be feared than any other danger. In any case, the southern route was shorter. It was obvious to me that nothing was going to dampen the optimism of our group. I knew the older men had no real concern about our safety, so with an almost uncontainable enthusiasm, we set out for Jerusalem, the City of God, the site of the temple, the home of God on earth.

I was in such high spirits that time seemed to fly. A lot of the children were my age—about seven of us were scattered throughout the camp—but Rachael, the daughter of a friend of my mother's, was the only one really close to me. Her appearance always seemed to bring a smile to my face. Her long, soft wool tunic, which had thin vertical stripes of bright orange, dull and dusty golds, and dark blues, with wider stripes of muted maroon edged with black, gray, and umber, so familiar to my people, at least in Nazareth, stirred deep and happy feelings. She was thin and lithe, and her long black hair was set off by even blacker eyes, which flashed a visible light, rising and falling in intensity with her mood and enthusiasm.

The only occasions when time seemed to slow down occurred when Rachael was close. Our eyes would meet on their random sweeps around the moving line of people, and often, she would sit beside me. We'd dangle our legs off the back of a cart or huddle down in the shade of the driver's seat to avoid the high sun. We didn't speak much, but we would smile and then look away, feeling a little guilty over the palpable, almost painful pleasure that rose through our bodies whenever we sat close together. Our accidental touching was so filled with sensations that they were indecipherable. We never would have been able to be so alone in the daily routine of our lives. It would have been forbidden to seek out such a time, and we never seemed to have occasion to be so close while simply going about the tasks of our young lives, but there, in the company of many adults, when everyone was attentive to the journey, our time together seemed like solitude. At night, I was perplexed that I was often thinking about her instead of anticipating the great moments just ahead when I would see the temple at last and pray to our God on his very doorstep. There came a moment I looked back upon many times over the next few years of my life, a moment when Rachael and I stared effortlessly into each other's eyes with no unease or shyness. Rather, we were so closely joined that although they were unspoken, words, sentences, thoughts, and feelings passed back and forth between us as if we were in afternoon discussion at the bazaar. This silent conversation held us before turning strangely painful, almost panicked, as our hands—which had, unknown to us, joined in perfect grip—were pulled apart. Our families returned to their places as we made the last great sweep around a line of hills that would bring us suddenly and imposingly into a position that afforded us our indelible first view of the temple.

I never saw Rachael again; her family moved to Judea within a month of our return, and I was told years later that she married a good and devoted man, a clerk who worked with the civil authorities, as did her father. I never forgot her, though, and even in the later stages of my human life, I thought about her when the pressures and disappointments of my life were hard upon me. But for the moment, there was no thought of such things. Each family had returned to its own position in the caravan, and the singular identity that had been our nature for the journey returned to the smaller units of households. Each family huddled together in prayer as we approached the moment the adults knew was soon to come.

And come it did. It was a fantastic sight. With the midmorning sun reflecting off the gilded walls, the temple was like a mountain of white when the eye could see past the bright golden fire that reflected from its heights. In all my studies, prayers, and wonder at the beauty of the natural world around me, nothing had prepared me for the grandeur of this sight, because it didn't seem to be of this earth. It looked like a union between heaven and earth, like God's glory coming from above, focused at this point, manifested in a celestial city from which poured a current of power nourishing and creating as it made its way down into the lower world. It puzzled me, in fact. As I sat with my family, with all our faces turned toward Jerusalem, all kinds of thoughts rushed through my mind. Was God indeed more involved in this world than I had come to believe? Did the imperfection and ignorance I had seen all around me as I grew in experience, dissipate as one approached this holy spot? Was there earthly perfection here, in stone and precious metal, and would the human custodians of this place also hold the clear reflection of truth as vehicles of the true Word of God?

The perception of transcendent glory hardly diminished as we grew nearer, but it became evident that the temple, as glorious as it had appeared from the distance, was of earthly nature. It was surrounded by solid walls showing a simple, massive face adorned only by the splendor of its size and pure white color and by the towers that showed its other nature as a fortress. The walls were uninterrupted in their great, smooth length except by the massive gates and heavy brass doors. I don't need to linger on the temple—it has been well described—but I want to explain the impact it had on me as a boy on the verge of manhood. I wanted the temple and all it stood for to be a holy place. I knew it had the blessing of the Creator Himself. Theoretically, it could house a clear and accurate source of truth, a sanctuary for a confused and violent world, a fountain of spiritual knowledge.

The temple had the potential to nourish first the Jews and later all the world during the dark hours of time as the massive conflict between two spiritual opposites ground its way toward resolution. It was the birthright of a chosen people, a people to whom God had extended his hand on all levels, and I had no reason to doubt that the temple stood in absolute similarity to true reality. Although the ethereal nature of the temple faded into the physical solidity of stone, wood, and polished metal, nothing I saw as we entered the great city made me question this hope, and it was with wholehearted enthusiasm and faith that I approached the God of Israel and his temple.

Over and above the splendor of the physical building, I was struck by the colorful streams of people who filled it. There were many, all dressed and adorned in the best they could manage, and where material lack might have impeded the ability to furnish a resplendent image, polished, clean, and carefully arranged attire made up the difference. We all smiled as our long days of comparative solitude evaporated into an ocean of moving, friendly humanity. It wasn't until after we had washed and refreshed ourselves to make our way through the gate and into the outer courtyard that I noticed the real poor, the beggars and the infirm, and the hawkers busy selling anything that might be needed for offering. We quickly found our lodgings. They were humble but clean and within the city gates, which was something even Jerusalem could not provide to all the thousands of visitors who came with Passover.

Magnificent is the best word for the temple. It continued to grow in splendor and size as we entered deeper into its heart. The first day, I was overwhelmed, capable of little but filling my eyes with the majestic images around me. As the festival went on, I adjusted to the grand scale, and although neither the awe nor the sensory joy I was so immersed in diminished, I found myself looking further, deeper. I was looking for something, some connection between the power I felt and the world of my own thoughts. It was hard to find. The prayer and ritual were little different from what I had been used to all my life, except in sheer size, and despite the imposing environment, my curiosity had not been satiated as I had hoped.

At the Passover dinner, my family formally vested me with the mantle of religious manhood.

It was a larger gathering than usual, for my parents had invited friends to make the night special—and it was. I'd always enjoyed the Passover celebrations, which brought out the best in us all, but that night, I was the recipient of more than my share of happiness. I was showered with kindness and affection. Gifts and advice were given with equal generosity. However, the next day wasn't as different as I had wanted it to be. I wasn't treated any differently, and I had no more opportunity to insert my own will into the daily activities than I'd had before. In the innocent naïveté of youth, I'd thought—and expected others to expect the same—I would now begin a new life as a true Son of the Commandment, as faithful young men were called, dedicating myself to our God and taking each and every action with God and his purpose firmly in mind. In fact, little changed. It was not until our traveling party began readying itself for the journey home that I found myself with more than a moment to myself. When I finally did find myself alone and able to do what I wanted, my mind prompted me to take advantage of where I was, the Holy City. I headed back toward the temple in serious contemplation and anxious to discover answers I would need before I continued with what was now officially my own destiny.

I made my way slowly through the crowd to the temple, walking and thinking. The sun was warm and pleasing. I was in no hurry, and I wanted to organize my thoughts and questions. I stopped under the covered colonnade that surrounded the large open courtyard. People of all types were there, mostly clustered in groups and locked in earnest conversation or listening while a self-appointed teacher explained an idea or a text that to him had a particular significance. It was easy to involve myself, and although the crowds had thinned with the end of the festival, the men remaining were a more garrulous group than the general crowd of worshippers the day before.

I joined one group after another, listening for a while to get the gist of the conversation and then politely interjecting a comment or two or posing a question to the man or men I thought most likely to have an answer or at least a response of interest. I soon realized that answers were not easy to come by; it was far more likely that my questions would lead to wider and wider circles to consider, with only scripture pulling us back to common ground. Time disappeared for me, and it was dark before I felt I had even scratched the surface of the knowledge I wanted to acquire before I returned to Nazareth. This was nothing like home. Everyone was in one spot: learned men obviously raised in the familiar doctrines and traditions and also Jews in finery unusual to my eye, their nobility present in voice and quality of thought. These imposing men scoffed at pharisaic doctrine as if it were illegitimate and less holy than the teachings of the princes and priests of Jerusalem with whom they identified. Men who were not Jews argued logically and adamantly for theologies as varied as variation itself, and some men spoke in quieter tones about revolt and intrigues I was familiar with but had never had the chance to listen to, much less discuss, in such depth and openness.

Some looked at me sharply when I spoke, but they soon turned back to the ebb and flow of words, knowing that a twelve-year-old Hebrew was probably as well trained as any adult of the nations and certainly formidable in terms of scripture. Scripture was the cornerstone of every subject being discussed within those walls. By the time darkness appeared, I had settled in with a group of about ten men. Our theme had distilled itself for the time being to the question of whether man's role in the world was to struggle and learn, strive and achieve, or passively place his fate in the hands of God without thought of a goal or a material measurement of success. I was startled out of my involvement by the darkness and the sudden thought of my parents, but as no one had come to search me out, I felt assured that my mother at least, fully aware of the responsibilities that came with religious adulthood, would understand that I must have been occupied in the pursuit of new understandings about how I should lead my life as a serious and devout man of God. Where else could I do that but there, within those walls and within God's presence? So I let my worries slip away and followed the group as we all moved toward a dining room beneath the cedar ceilings of the colonnade. We ate and talked, until I slipped to the floor and wrapped myself in the soft wool blanket one of my new friends passed to me just moments before I fell into a deep and contented sleep.

In the morning, I awoke with a great eagerness to plunge into the day. I washed and ate with the group of travelers who remained from last night's discussions, and then I made my way to a more serene spot to pray and meditate. After a mental review of all that had been said the day before, I realized I wasn't satisfied with what I had learned. I saw that the ideas and topics we'd talked about, as stimulating and refreshing as the atmosphere had been, were not much different from what we talked about in school or during the Sabbath afternoons spent with my family and friends. Certainly the lack of consensus was familiar.

I had to shake my head when I thought about how virtually any subject not fully accepted as canon seemed to have an equal number of equally smart men defending opposite sides of the question. That wasn't what I wanted; I wanted real wisdom from men who had lived to see the absoluteness of that wisdom—wisdom I could use to make decisions about how to conduct the rest of my life. I wasn't going to get that from the arguments of speculation, so I headed deeper into the temple to find a more unified and enlightened source of advice and counsel. I passed, as we had done just days ago, through the crowded courtyard into the smaller and holier area where the men worshiped and the priests made sacrifice. I found a corner away from the crowds and knelt to pray, meditate, and then observe.

I watched for at least a couple of hours, until I noticed that the flow of activity divided itself. The priests went about their tasks with somber certainty, receiving and attending to the larger offerings. They lent each action the importance it held for the family, who might have traveled hundreds of miles to express their dedication to God. I also noticed that discreetly, almost strategically, placed throughout the narrow courtyard were several groups of older men who did not appear to be priests but who, it was equally evident, had a familiarity and comfort with the holy room that could only have come from years of habitual occupation. As I watched, I saw that they were reading from scrolls. They were not continuously focused on their reading as a student anxious to finish and move on to his next assignment would have been; they read, with great calm and consideration, a few verses or even pages and then paused for contemplation and consideration of what they had just read, although, again, it seemed obvious they were familiar with every word. Occasionally, three or four would engage in conversation, usually referring back to and rereading aloud some portion of the text within a page or two of what they had just read. This format was nothing new to me, as the elder men of the synagogue often sat and did just so, but there was a difference here. Unlike with the elders of Nazareth, there was a persistent calm among the men. It would have been unusual to observe the thinkers of my town reading and discussing scripture without the obligatory and frequent escalation of what had been a conversation to an animated and usually noisy debate complete with gestures and enthusiasm that skirted the edges of anger.

I quietly moved myself within earshot and sat. I listened for what seemed a long time—a few hours, I suppose. I couldn't make out every word, but I did hear enough to know, basically, what they were talking about. It was like cool water on a sore. Although the tumble of words I had sorted through yesterday was important, it had been more effective in eliminating questions than answering them. There was a new clarity today, a focus that brought awareness of what I needed to know and what I already knew. I now knew, for instance, that armed struggle was not the path of a godly man.Despite the carefully argued rationalizations that had such appeal to our nationalism and our material wishes, there was no real scriptural support for such a path. It was clear that after the destruction of Solomon's temple, the nation that had once existed with the direct support of God would not truly rise again until the end of the gentile times, until the end of the world and the beginning of a new world, and that both the end and the beginning would be brought about by the spiritual power of God himself from above. No band of sword- wielding zealots, no matter how fierce or well intentioned, was to bring that about.

I think all truly religious men of my time knew that, but men being men, it was hard to accept that we, as the true people of God, would remain under the heel of the great and unholy power of Rome. Being able to discuss those things continuously and intensely had rolled what I had learned in my young life into a long band. I saw what I knew and what I did not know, and as I approached one of the circles of wise men, feeling the palpable presence of consciousness that surrounded them like a soft rain, I felt I could learn what I still needed to know.

It was late afternoon by the time I made my first comment to that learned group. I received some long and penetrating glances from a few of the bearded and robed mountains, but no one appeared surprised or provoked by my immediate presence. I summoned my courage and asked a question that related to the topic they had been discussing for more than an hour. I received a reply that seemed to continue with the nature and direction of their conversation, and with that comfort and unspoken acceptance, I sat back, figuratively, within myself and breathed a sigh of relief and pleasure, preparing myself to try to shape that lofty conversation into the form of the Teacher I needed.

It seemed as if only a few minutes had gone by, when the words simply ceased. There was prayer, and then our collective attention went to the priests and the altar. It was a sudden reminder of the great and wonderful dream of which I was a part. My eyes lifted up to the huge mass of unhewn stones that formed the altar and beyond to the great height of the face of the holy house adorned with gold and carved shapes, where even then, as flame, smoke, and glorious music rose in sacred unison, the priests dissolved behind the curtained entrance to the most holy, bringing the day of sacrifice to a solemn close. I sat and allowed my body and mind to absorb as much of the sensory feast as I could, and I gave my own burning thanks to a God who filled my heart as much as he filled the universe around me. Almost involuntarily, my body rose and moved into the outer courtyards, where I talked, ate, and slept in a light-filled trance, falling off to sleep as candlelight flickered around me and the soft rise and fall of human voices soothed me to sleep as gently and effectively as my mother's arms.

The morning, however, was bright and clear, and although the images of yesterday's pageantry tried to show themselves as dreams, I knew they were not, and I was soon clean and filled with enough food and enthusiasm to walk to the altar of Jehovah for the morning sacrifice.

I found the same group assembled, as if they had not moved at all, and when I sat, as I had done the day before, several of the men closest to me greeted me by name with kindness and even affection. Soon we were once again a little universe of our own, plotting our informal but definite course across the immense backdrop of truth and knowledge. But that day was slightly different, tracking a wider circle than the one we'd traversed the day before.

It was well understood that we, the children of Israel, were in a tough spot. We were alone in a world that was fundamentally dark, spiritually divided and distorted, and inherently without the ability to extract itself from a degraded and violent reality.

We agreed that a day of deliverance, a day of final judgment and ultimate peace, with transcendence over death a part of that peace, was to come to the world. The keepers of the temple also agreed that the Day of God was literal and would not come before the appearance of the Messiah, the prophesied Savior of Israel and of the world. His appearance was to occur in Israel—and soon. I was surprised those men were in anticipation of the arrival of the Savior even as we spoke, and I was pleased and surprised that most of the men held that whatever force was to be used to restore the kingdom of God would be spiritual in nature and would be wielded in God's name by the Messiah and his heavenly army alone. Mankind would be a passive recipient of that great transformation.

I tried to steer the discussion in the courtyard toward those topics, and I found little resistance; in fact, my wise friends seemed most inclined to talk about the plight and expectations of the children of God. However, there was also a peripheral aspect of our discussions that gave me equal substance to think about over the next few years. I noticed that when we followed the scriptures to their heart concerning what really was to happen in our lifetimes and the life of mankind itself, the harmonious unity of thought that was so powerful and pleasant began to fray. When I asked in the precociousness of youth for more specific details about when and where the Messiah was to manifest himself and who he was, or when I wondered how the divergences between the temple priests and the teachings of the synagogues could be resolved or why the name of God was apparent in fewer of the scrolls used at the temple than in the villages, I was often surprised to find myself sitting quietly while three or four of my mentors argued points and theories less and less relevant to the scriptures and more and more subjective—and in tones and manners much more similar to the bickering that had puzzled me in the gates and markets of Nazareth. After one such minor disagreement, as the faces and voices returned to more loving countenances and reasoned tones, I heard the voice of my father at my shoulder. Whatever was left of my dreamlike state vanished as I looked up and, in an instant, saw that he was not pleased with me. It seemed only a moment until I was before my mother, standing just outside the entrance that denied her access to the altar, explaining to her that I honestly had been doing what I thought I should.

On some level, I knew she agreed with me, and we said little as we made our way back to the small party that had turned around from its path home to find me. No one was really angry, but I learned another subtlety of the melding of the law with life. Although I was now an individual and responsible for my thoughts and actions, I was still very much a part of the family, and due to my age, I had to respect my parents' wishes when it came to my whereabouts and activities.

Chapter Three

I was glad to get home, but the sheer immenseness of the trip on every level, made it something I thought about for a long time. My memories of the temple stayed with me. That first sight of it shining like a white-and-gold mountain fit so seamlessly with what I imagined God's point of contact with the earth would be like that in a way, it became a timeless image, a glimpse of a time to come.

In my mind, I went over and over the conversations with the men of the temple courtyard. I could remember virtually every word; the subjects and sequences of the dialogue had seemed almost predictable as we slid back and forth along the well-measured landscape of our faith. Although I was familiar with most of the references we'd used as architecture for our thoughts and words, I had made a few mental notes to study the more esoteric references made by the older men, references that showed a depth of understanding and familiarity with scripture that was obviously more evolved than even the most knowledgeable of the local wise men. Especially in Daniel, Ezekiel, and Isaiah, I had been given a glimpse of prophetic meaning that had not been evident to me in our local studies.

With this scholastic catching up to do and feeling the welcome burden of the higher expectations my family and community now had for me as a young adult, the next few years passed happily and productively. By the time I was fourteen, or certainly fifteen, I really was a help to my father, and I could only smile at myself for having thought I always had been. We both worked hard. I loved the work, perhaps even more now that I produced things that translated into real value for my family. The satisfaction I had knowing that we prospered—in a simple and limited way, true, but we prospered nonetheless—not insignificantly due to my own efforts, allowed me freedom to enjoy myself in other ways when the time I had was undisputedly my own and well deserved. I felt sorrow for others who did not have that simple source of happiness, the joy that came from a loving family, worthwhile work, and simple faith, but I knew, even at fifteen, that the deep malignancy of the world was ruthless in the things it denied many of its people, often taking away the opportunity for happiness even before they knew they had it. But I had it, and I knew it; and my perfect instincts kept me from making mistakes that could have ruined it.

I would walk into the nearby hills late in the afternoon and fill myself with pleasure—not often ecstasy but pleasure. It was beautiful there. The desert flowers supplied the nose with scents that often made the mouth burst out in appreciation, and the twilight, as it wrapped me and the world around me in a blanket of color and feeling that made us one, was magic. This alchemy was a residue of the presence of God, not some lower occult that sprang from and led to emptiness. I had a lot of simple pleasures and busy days, and they easily rolled themselves into months and years.

When I returned to Nazareth from the Passover at Jerusalem, I was a boy, despite the fact that I had been formally initiated into manhood, but over the next few years I grew into the world of physical manhood. By fifteen, I was tall and was interested in girls, especially the girls who were turning into women just as I was a man. Among my people, the pull of the flesh was not something young adults had to deal with on their own. Everyone talked about it. In fact, everyone delighted in talking about it. When a boy was about fourteen, his mother would begin to plague him about it, saying, for example, "What do you think about young Miriam, my cousin's girl? Isn't she wonderful?" or "Remember, Son, a good wife is a rare treasure. You should think about that," or "How will you ever get a good wife if you behave like that? Do you want to end up lonely and childless like your uncle Judah?" Fathers were not much better, saying, "Don't be deceived by a pretty face, my boy. That will fade soon enough, and all you will be left with is a sharp and bitter tongue," or "Don't be too anxious to marry. I can tell you these are the best years for you."

Of course, as new adults, most of us liked the attention and the topic, as much as we squirmed and shook our heads. But we thought about it too, and by the age when we were beginning to assist in the duties of the synagogue, we sometimes found ourselves staring a little too long at some pretty face or being suddenly entranced by the happy voice of an excited girl talking much longer than expected about something that all at once seemed much more worthy of consideration, even though we didn't really understand or care exactly what she was talking about. It was interesting. I know I've said this before, and it is no accident that I say it again; it was God that was important to us. We had learned and accepted that from the time we were barely talking, and it was easy to accept because we saw that faith being worked out by our parents, our neighbors, our town, and our nation. Despite the hardships imposed by the outside world, it was easy to see that this truth was real indeed. It worked. It nurtured and protected us; it gave us joy, and it gave us strength. Although the rulers of our faith sometimes made it hard not to resist or even resent the sometimes harsh restraints, unwanted interference, or petty judgments that caused doubt and even pain, the common man knew his faith was good, and despite the often apparent faults, there was an underlying power and truth to our religion that we never forgot.

So the young had little confusion about marriage. We knew we would have it. We thought about it and planned for it. We anticipated, and were often impatient for, the fulfillment of our passions, but we also knew we had to do it correctly or suffer. We were under no illusion that male–female love was the single transcendent ingredient needed for happiness. We knew that marriage was part of the fabric of our faith and simply a stone—a cornerstone, yes, but just one stone—in the structure that was our life. Physical love did not rise to the level of a cornerstone. We knew what it was but not clearly, and it was not really discussed; it was something one might hope for but could not expect. Like every town, Nazareth had its all too visible examples of human tragedy, whether caused by selfish male opportunism or foolish female disregard. Our ability to be patient with our hearts and avoid mistakes was made possible by the fact that we simply were not given the chance to make mistakes or to act impulsively. By the age of puberty, boys and girls were not allowed to be alone together. Our parents not only were good at telling us why, when, and if but also watched us like hawks. My moments of emotional and mental intimacy with Rachael had come amid a crowd, and if one of the adults had fully noticed, we would have been deftly but kindly separated or at least joined in our reverie by an adult.

I went along with the tide, not making any decisions or drawing any conclusions about romance. After the shock of being told she was gone, I thought about Rachael a lot, and I felt pain at her absence, but by the time I was fifteen, she seemed to cross my mind only on rare occasions, and when she did, I felt more warmth than pain. I was in no hurry to replace her with another, although I did wish I might find myself gazing into eyes as captivating as hers by simple circumstance or coincidence. However, I had another area of interest.

As I mentioned, I got great enjoyment from walking in the quiet places. By the time I was eighteen or so, I knew the land around Nazareth so well I could walk for miles without ever having to wonder where I was going, so I never had to hurry. I could sit and look. I could close my eyes, breathe, and open them again to smile at the beauty around me.

God was certainly present but in a quiet and subtle way. I never had much in the way of adventure spiritually or otherwise, but I had a gentle peace that bound the daily activities of my life into a slowly filling awareness. By the time I was in my early twenties, I felt big. I was fully grown, and I appreciated my strength and my feeling of comfort with my world. My time alone left me practiced at meditation, and the confines of contemplation began to yield a deeper and brighter light, one that brought with it a vague restlessness.

More and more, when I made my way home after an afternoon or evening in the hills, I noticed a curious division of perception.

There was a surface layer I saw with my senses that seemed complete, smooth, and fully in harmony with my thoughts and my concepts of what life was, but I often found myself startled by how that surface cracked when I engaged in physical contact with things that apparently had a deeper will of their own. A leather bag or a piece of food could suddenly appear separate, or foreign even, to my touch and sight, causing me to draw back and find myself in a slightly different world that was separate and fragmented, small and sharp, whereas an instant before, it had been whole and vast. The feeling was most evident when someone spoke to me or when I listened to the conversation of others as I rejoined my village. Sometimes the feeling was so strong that when a friend or even a family member spoke to me, his or her words and the resulting ripples of meaning that penetrated my own surprisingly delicate fabric of reality would almost feel like an assault on the invisible cords of feeling within me, and I would have to look away, smiling to disguise the unexpected effects of the person's simple comments.

I gave up trying to protect the fragile calm that came from isolation. There was no way to avoid natural contact with people— or things, for that matter—who obviously had no inherent malice toward me. They were simply my life, but I was surprised at how separate the world could be from my own internal peace.

I was twenty-four when my father died. His death was sudden, and it shocked us all. By that time, I had four brothers and two sisters, and we all took for granted and depended on the quiet goodness of Joseph. All men mourn, so I have little to say about the months after his death. As the oldest, I had to place my sorrow behind the unexpected responsibilities I now had. I didn't have to think about changing; I simply changed. I embraced my mother with all my strength and faith. I held my brothers and sisters with newfound force, keeping the empty spaces filled with work and prayer and trying to allow our tears to merge and lose themselves in the long history of sorrow we held as a people. We had faith, and the deep wisdom and hitherto untapped strength of my mother gave solace and peace to us all.

Any unborn thoughts I might have had about my growing curiosity and restlessness concerning my future disappeared. I took over the workshop and the tasks that went along with having to see that our family would not suffer materially. I journeyed to the villages and merchants that had supplied my father with wood and to the markets and families that bought what we made. I learned to talk, bargain, sit with the men at the gates, and eat and drink with them, not just feeling the joy of discussing our faith and our future but also knowing that at the end of the day, I could expect old customers to clasp my arm and offer their fraternity to a new family head, a man like them, with a silent oath of shared needs and burdens. Long walks with their accompanying questions about the nature of what was and what was to come became rare for the first few years after Joseph passed. As the pain subsided, I allowed myself more freedom, and I began to return to some of my old solitudes, surprised to find a familiar cave or cluster of trees unchanged in its ability to offer shade and the sweet light of spiritual retreat.

Once again, I sought time alone in prayer, meditation, and simple idyll, and I found the separation between the world of my aloneness and the world of my role as a man was more distinct than ever. It no longer shocked me to find the bright, singing universe I carried with me as I walked toward the village knocked and buffeted into a resigned but familiar normality. But that difference led me to look forward all the more to the times I had by myself. My study had progressed, and the puzzlement and wonder I'd once held at the depth of scriptural knowledge displayed by the wise teachers at the temple long ago had been replaced by simple appreciation for the power and wisdom of the holy texts. That wisdom formed the basis of my meditation. I had found the thread of secrets that circled its way through the Word of God, and I was more and more in anticipation of what was to come. I didn't think of myself as unique or special, but I knew how special mankind inherently was. I saw that the revealing of that potential was something to come, prophesied by men of the past and demanding of men of the present, and I looked forward to making my contribution to that revelation of our divine nature. I had learned from men both historical and contemporary. Even in Nazareth were men, unheralded and seemingly unlikely men, who had come to see a hidden depth to the world of the senses and had slipped away from the benefits of prominence to the hidden rewards of introspection and dedication to the search for a conscious awareness of the Living God. I had made a point of sitting and talking to those men. They all shared excitement about the times we lived in, certain that great things were going to happen and eager to share their certainty. It reinvigorated them to pass on what they knew or thought. I knew something was going on beneath the surface, but I had no inclination to withdraw from daily life. At twenty-eight, I had clear obligations, and whatever truth had in store, it lay enfolded in the fact that my family needed me.

Sarah and I knew each other, being children of families that had slightly intersecting orbits, but it seemed we met for the first time on a day preceding the Sabbath. Late in the afternoon, as I made my way back to my family to prepare for the evening meal, I was happy and filled with the spirit of my own world when I saw her. She was undoubtedly on her way home, as I was. As we approached, our eyes met, and she spoke my name in polite greeting. She was smiling, and I realized there were no sharp corners to the sound of her voice or the wave of her thoughts. In fact, I felt a familiarity with the sound and quality of her voice that belied the depth of our relationship. We just smiled at each other, with no inclination to avert our eyes or stop the motion of the shared spirit that grew between us. I saw Rachael in her face, and then I saw Sarah. I knew I should have been self- conscious about the joy I was feeling at the nearness and intensity of her beauty, but whatever reticence I might have had was swept away in the force of the feeling. We just stared until her face was framed in light, and I looked away. Her name finally escaped my lips, and I reached for her hand.

We walked silently for a few steps, until the approaching darkness reminded us that we had to go. To say I was content as I walked the short distance to my home would be an understatement. My immediate future seemed clear as I tried to sort out the blaze of emotions that occupied my mind and heart. I could not ignore my responsibility to my family, and if I were to remain there in Nazareth to look after my mother and my younger siblings, it seemed only natural and fitting that I be married. At that moment, I wanted nothing else.

The next morning, I told my mother about Sarah. She was smiling and attentive as I tried to explain my new feelings. I don't recall what she said, but I knew she was bursting with happiness when she hugged me and assured me she knew exactly how to proceed. It was not long before I found myself at Sarah's family's table, eating and joining in the festive mood of the meal, enjoying the curious glances of her sisters, and feeling a kind of pride that they seemed pleased with our new interest in each other.

The next few months went by happily and predictably. Since Sarah and I were older than most of the young people who displayed the symptoms of romance, we were pretty much left alone to get to know each other at our own pace. Both families knew we were loyal to our beliefs, and no one, including ourselves, had any fears about our ability to control our evident passion.

Sarah was everything I could have wanted. She was as beautiful as her namesake and as striking for her calm confidence and spiritual strength as for her beauty. I took her with me on walks to the most accessible and inspiring of my rural haunts, and we spent as much time as we could talking about the things that were important to us and enjoying the magnitude of what we had, not surprisingly, in common.

I suppose we would have married within a year or two. But something happened. We were talking, as we always seemed to be, with words and thoughts flowing along lines as parallel as the tracks of a cart, when we suddenly found ourselves silent. Sarah knew the Word of God. I wasn't surprised by her knowledge, knowing her family and our traditions, but it was a source of great joy for me that she could speak so clearly about our faith and share with me the subtleties of truth in a way I found faultless. Perhaps that was why I was surprised at our impasse. I had been speaking about our life, my enthusiasm for a future certain to be filled with the mystery and power of God, and how I looked forward to a time when our world would be replaced by the true reality, a reality that would show our present life to be the shadow that it was. I suppose, in retrospect, I had never spoken that way to anyone, and although the thought was a common one to me, it had always been confined to internal dialogue. Even though everything I said was commonly accepted as part of our faith, I could see that to her, it was a shock. Whether due to destiny, overzealousness, or lack of context, for us, it was not well said. Even after I rephrased my comments, we were no closer to agreement. "What is so wrong with the world we have, Jesus?" She said. "I know that our world isn't perfect, but we need to have faith in God, and if we're good, things will work out."

I calmed myself and grew more serious. "Sarah, I know that this world holds a lot of beauty and that happiness is a thing to be sought after, but doesn't God make it clear in scripture that it is in a new world that we will find peace?"

"But it's not up to us, Jesus, to make that happen." So it went.

I tried my best to explain to her that I agreed with her, but for honesty's sake, I had to add that although faith was necessary and good, like the prophets before us, a man had to be willing to do what God required in order to make a contribution to the unfolding of God's will upon the earth, even if that meant sacrifice. Soon she was silent. I could see disbelief in her mind. I watched as she thought about her children yet to come and saw her recoil at the image of a husband who might put them all in danger simply for the sake of speaking out, of making a fuss and being rebellious. I felt joy leave my body. I couldn't believe it. There, invading that most cherished of moments, was the same old shard of separation that had disrupted my sense of oneness so many times before. There in the intimacy of a bond I had been so comfortable with, in a love that felt so natural and good that our closeness should have lasted forever, was a vast rift. It seemed unfair to me that we had been brought together by circumstance and common intention —by destiny, it seemed—only to arrive at that subtle but fiercely immovable difference of opinion. As we left each other that day, feeling awkward but hopeful tomorrow would set things straight, I started to face something I had ignored for a long time. Perhaps the obedience I felt to God was not shared by the natural direction of my life. I had always managed an uneasy truce between memories of my mother's words telling of a sacred heritage, a kingship from the House of David, and the daily reality of my life. That truce allowed perhaps that those ideas were simply metaphorical and would reveal themselves as symbols of spiritual goals pursued and gained. However, war had come to that previously unchallenged peace. I felt an unwanted certainty grow within me that adherence to what I saw clearly as the right thing to do—following the will of God—was going to move me further and further apart from the path I would have chosen if I'd concerned myself only with the needs of the physical man. This contradicted the assumption I'd previously held that I lived in a world where doing the right thing materially was synonymous with doing the right thing spiritually. Of course, such harmony is how it should be in the world; it's how we try to make it and even how it is for some men sometimes. But the true source of pain for all men is that we are separated from such integration, regardless of how well we behave or how lucky we are.

Within a few days of our uneasy parting, I knew I could never marry. Marriage to me would have been unfair to any woman because of the pain I now knew my life would bring to her. I thought I understood, in a broad sense, what my life required of me. No human could see the path I had to walk without a perfect nature of his or her own, and even Sarah did not have that capability. She would have been torn apart by conflict and doubt over what was to happen, unsure of herself and unsure of me, a victim of agonies that were unnecessary if I simply bore them myself, substituting solitude for solace. That dawning awareness brought me the deepest pain of my life, for, from the moment of that realization, I was alone. I was always alone. I had no hesitation; in fact, I embraced the idea that I must redefine the conflict between comfort and faith if faith required it, but there was a terrible sickness of heart in knowing I could never ask that same sacrifice from someone who would become one with me in flesh.

However, I knew what to do, and I knew without insecurity that it was the right thing to do, so the pain became simply a part of my life, like a handicap that I bore but didn't dwell upon again.

I could ask for love from the position of teacher and friend and accept love as a teacher and friend, but I could never subject a woman to physical union, when the inevitable pain would fall so unevenly on her.

I had no real awareness in terms of understandable images of who I was or what was to come. I was growing. I functioned perfectly, and thus, I had no real reason to manifest what I knew in words or thoughts. The mind is the part of the body that joins the physical with the spiritual. Working properly, it does the bidding of the individual spirit of each man. If spirit is silenced or subverted, the mind operates the body based on what it has learned to that point, unable to take advantage of new spiritual intuition and, thus, unable to avoid error. Each man has spirit that is confined to his own body; it belongs to him and allows him to operate as a creature of both the seen and unseen worlds. Being of the same nature as the Spirit of God, the spirit of each man has the capability, through the oneness of all spirit, to take direction, knowledge, and strength from the spirit of the universe and thrive in the world of time and space.

When I observed the world, I had knowledge through spirit of what I saw, what it meant, what it was, and what was to come, but that knowledge did not become thought until it needed to or until I directed my conscious inquiry toward it. When I looked at people, I saw them. But I more than saw them: I could also feel their condition. I did not think about it, but in my vision, I saw and understood any part of their spirit that was not in harmony with the spirit of the universe around them. Most of the time, that difference was not brought into awareness, for all men had separation from the perfect spirit, so to my sight, the person was simply a man or a woman. However, if the aberration was large enough or strong enough, it would stand out and catch my attention. I knew what it was even as I looked, and if I focused, the knowledge that existed in spirit would translate, through the mind, into thought and then symbols as words. The words might be of pain, anger, confusion, or hatred, but they brought to consciousness a knowledge already shared by my spirit and the Spirit of God. We all operate like this, and I know many of you know this, but the point I want to make is that at that time in my life, I did not know in a verbal, cerebral sense what was to happen in the future or even what was happening in the moment. But I did have a silent knowledge—knowledge in light, you might say—of both, and I rested in and relied on that consciousness, the faith that is present in the silence of perception.

Within a month of my realization that marriage was not a possibility, my attention shifted to what that meant, and spirit began to bring the answer into awareness. As the awareness grew, it subtly altered the reality around me. I looked upon my family and saw that things had changed. Time had healed the wounds of Joseph's death as much as such wounds could heal, and two of my brothers had grown to mature men. If I envisioned them without me, I saw that they would be perfectly able to look after my mother and my sisters. That was a bit of a surprise because I had felt such a burden of responsibility for them all, and although I had looked forward to that responsibility, I now saw that my life was not going to unfold as I had expected. I knew my mother was distraught as the realization that I was not going to marry Sarah sank in, for she shared the question of what my future held, and she was worried.

Things went along normally for a while, but one day, as spring approached, my mother drew me aside, asking me to sit with her in the warm sun of the early afternoon. "You know your cousin has been preaching in the desert, Jesus, and now he is at the River Jordan. Everyone's talking about him; he is drawing people from the cities and calling for us all to repent because the events of heaven are revealing themselves. What do you think he's doing?" I stalled a little; I wasn't ready to relate what John was doing to my own life. She persevered, and I answered, surprised a little by my own words. She looked at me in silence and then said in a voice that allowed no doubt, "Go, Jesus. Go to him, and begin what you were born to do. I have done all I can." By the end of summer, I was gone.

Chapter Four

I took little with me. I walked along the ridge of the hills, and by nightfall, I was in land that was unfamiliar, although I knew it would lead down into the valley that skirted the hills and would wind south and east toward the Jordan.

In the morning it seemed as if I were a different person. I had no thoughts of the past. As I looked at my arms and legs I felt a sense of seeing things for the first time. Inside, I was the same. I mean the overall texture of my nature seemed the same, but the world was different. The vastness of the horizon seemed more immediate, and my vision based its images more on light than on form; with that came a blurring of the lines between my own body and the world around me. I was intensely alive yet strangely light, seeming almost to flow rather than walk. The feeling diminished as time passed. Sometimes the exertion of a climb and the heat it brought with it sharpened the foreground and made my body more substantial, intensifying the feeling and color of my clothing and my skin, as if I had gained in density and mass. Sometimes the feeling of the staff in my hand held my attention just beneath the effort of searching ahead for the path. What had been inert as a piece of wood was now charged with energy, seeming to change back and forth from near weightlessness to a heavy solidity that pulled and pointed in one direction or another as if attached to the world around it by an invisible force. I was not unfamiliar with any of those sensations, but they were exaggerated from anything I had felt before and had a new feeling of importance, of urgency.

I didn't feel as if I wanted to see anyone right away, until I felt comfortable with myself and more certain of what I was doing, so I took a long time to reach the river. I spent more and more time sitting and thinking, watching the world as my thoughts played in and out of my mind. What was I doing?

I thought about my life. I prayed. I waited. I thought, and I prayed again. After a while, I saw the pattern. I went back and forth over the events that rose in my memory, until nothing new interjected itself to interrupt the overall view. I didn't know why I should be different from anyone else, but I also realized no one knew why they were confined within themselves, separate. I knew there was a God. I knew there was a world beyond our own and greater than our own. I knew a time would come when that greater world would impose itself upon the earth and require us to harmonize with a reality that reflected the true nature of God. I knew we waited for that. I knew there was a role for me to play in it, and when I was honest with myself, I knew it was to be a role that would bring me close to God and to his will, as his son.

As I rose from that conclusive meditation, the final thoughts were still speaking, forming. I had to accept my path, and I vowed, even as I reached for my pack and continued down toward the area where I expected John to be, to embrace it fully and not look back.

The force of my resolve brought about enthusiasm, and I smiled a little foolishly, as men do when they surrender themselves to the Living God and feel the warmth of his acceptance and approval. I walked slowly now, letting the fullness and beauty of each moment rise and fall in body, mind, and heart.

I walked south along the western bank of the Jordan, sometimes winding up into the hills so that the river was out of sight, but always, my path returned within sight of the water. After some time, I crossed the river at a spot that I could see would be relatively easy. I knew from local gossip that John had been preaching in the country around the river and that on the eastern side, a few days' walk from the Sea of Galilee, he had settled in, baptizing Jews in large numbers as they poured out from Judea and Galilee to hear his message, a message that was resonating with the people of Israel and causing much speculation as to who this man was and what, if anything, his sudden rise to prominence meant.

I hadn't seen my cousin for almost twenty years, perhaps because the dramatic events that had occurred at the time John and I were born weighed invisibly but heavily over both Mary and Elizabeth. It wasn't until I knew I was leaving Nazareth that my mother and I even discussed the prophecies made concerning John when he was born. I was sure the disconcertingly consistent way in which the predictions were playing out had made her draw on her deepest memories to relive and remind me of the time in her life when she was visited by angels. It had been a time when faith, love, and life were imposed against the brilliant light of eternity. The spirit of God had made itself known to her, and the result of that transcendent union had yielded my life. It had been difficult for her to believe that the angel Gabriel really was the angel Gabriel when he spoke to her, but the truth speaks in a fair language. There have always been some who can recognize the speech of the universal tongue, for that part of us which is from God knows God. But to accept into full awareness the fact that you are to be mother to the Son of God, a man destined to rule over all Israel in a supernatural fashion, is beyond the ability of any mortal, and it was Spirit that held my mother free from any conflicts of mind and spirit, as befit the purity, power, and dignity of the things that had taken place. However, the intensity of the events surrounding my birth some thirty years before had been short-lived. By the time I was five, Life had become life for my mother. Spectral words and thoughts, even holy ones, are by nature rare and soon lose their solidity in the progress of time. So it was with her.

But then, there was John. I have spoken about John before, but I want to elaborate a little. I was rethinking those matters as I walked toward our reunion. Elizabeth and Mary were separated by years, Elizabeth being the elder and, in their youth, the more ascendant of the two. Although Elizabeth and Mary were raised together in the extended family, Elizabeth's parents were wealthy and prominent, rich in faith as well as earthly goods. Elizabeth and Mary loved each other, sharing a kindred affection based perhaps on the sincerity of faith common to both girls, and Elizabeth and my mother were inseparable. Consequently, the girls were educated together, with Mary benefiting from the high training Elizabeth required to fulfill her parents' desire that she marry a righteous and influential man. The intensity of their religious training went well with both women, and they shared a faith and passion that held the admiration of all they met. They were both dedicated to the God of Israel with the full force of their joy and power as well as with their considerable beauty and intelligence. Marriage would only be a deeper commitment to their religion and the truth, for in our traditions, asceticism, especially for a woman, was normally the path of the weak, not the strong. It was an intense time for them, with their faith playing out in that uncommon earthly occurrence wherein the confluences of earth and spirit come together and great Work is done. They felt that, and the bond between them became a spiritual one; they were sisters approaching the bright throne of eternity, walking hand in hand, excited and filled with joy, as their path spiraled ever closer to the golden center.

Auspicious event followed auspicious event, and when Elizabeth married Zechariah, a handsome older man who was a respected and admired priest, it seemed earth and heaven were one for her, for she loved him almost as intensely as her faith.

The marriage tested the girls' relationship, of course, but Mary was able to live with the new household for a long time, and the new role Elizabeth adopted as wife had plenty of room for female companionship and shared duties. However, Elizabeth was getting older by childbearing standards, and still, no child had come; it appeared she was barren. Although unspoken, it was a terrible strain, casting a communal doubt on her relationship with God, that he not favor her with the child both families so desired and expected. Nonetheless, both women remained strong in faith and strong in friendship, certain that the spirit of life was real in their lives, incapable of fostering anything but the will of the Creator.

It wasn't until Mary, then in her twenties, was betrothed to Joseph, who was an upright and faithful man but poor compared to the upper echelons of the priesthood Zechariah occupied, that a real separation occurred. Mary would go to live in Nazareth; Elizabeth would remain in more noble dwellings in Judea.

They prayed and held each other, weeping and promising never to let anything come between their sacred friendship but knowing they would slip further and further from each other as the currents of their disparate futures moved on.

It seemed their shared vision of spiritual fulfillment would fade into good but different, separate, and more mundane lives. However, they were determined, and within a year of their separation, held together in prayer and faith, both were rewarded in ways that seldom come to even the most persevering of seekers. No more than the most fortunate of men have direct contact with spiritual beings in their mortal lives, for this only occurs when it is necessary in some way for the outworking of this world's tragic path to deliverance. Fortunate were both Mary and Elizabeth. John's birth was predicted and proclaimed by the angel Gabriel, who both named him and promised that he was to be a man great in the eyes of God, with the power and spirit of Elijah to turn the hearts of men back to God. Then there were the even more far-reaching and absolute prophecies about me. Every possible dream of both Mary and Elizabeth was realized by the time of my birth, but those realizations proved the beginning of the end for the almost dreamlike years of intensity, faith, and spirit they had shared. My mother's visit to Elizabeth in her sixth month of pregnancy signaled a triumphant end to the time of their great sisterhood, and they moved with great happiness into a future that portended to be more than they could have imagined.

Their lives proceeded with nothing to suggest that the future held less than had been foretold, but as the years passed without any real impact or influence from the miracles, their need for such extraordinary underpinnings also diminished. Neither woman was the type to boast or remind others of what had happened, and as their children grew, the events of the past took on an almost academic tone. For Elizabeth, that did not mean she did not use the past as an incentive for John to excel, for both she and her husband were of the priesthood: Elizabeth was a direct descendant of the house of Aaron, and Zechariah was an active priest in the temple of Jehovah. Zechariah had been given instructions directly from Gabriel regarding how to raise John and the nature of his future, and since the verity of the angel's words had been punctuated by Zechariah being struck with blindness until the child's birth—a reminder that a priest should not doubt his faith—both parents brought John up to take his place as a prophet of God. They did not fully appreciate the way John manifested his destiny: by choosing the desert rather than the temple, choosing ascetic purity rather than tradition, and offending many with his direct and relentlessly serious nature. John, in fact, had become a worry to his parents by the time of his late adolescence, rejecting the formality and security of the temple, preferring to spend long periods of time in the desert, fasting, and having little to do with the affairs of men. He was charismatic and engaging but in a way that brought his parents a little more concern than contentment. However, John was progressing in the training of a priest, and that satisfied them, at least until he was thirty. It was then expected that he take up his post at the temple as a novice priest, but instead, John returned to the desert and began to rail against both the people of Israel and their priesthood.

It wasn't until the word had spread that John was preaching with an intensity that recalled old miracles, attracting multitudes of first curious and then repentant Jews into the wild desert, that mother began to see that another chapter was opening. She knew all too well that the "One" John talked about coming behind him was me, and if that were true, so was the immensity of what lay ahead. So it was that she told me everything she knew—every word, every astonishing event that concerned either John or me— and sent me out to meet him and my destiny.

Now I was looking down on a scene that seemed to strand me in time, as if I had stood on that spot for an eternity.

It was a place where the water of the Jordan spilled out into the desert, down a ravine lined with hills, where it joined a large pool created by an underground spring. The northern side of the pool was dense with reeds, but on the south the water formed a small lagoon that stretched up against the soft, rounded dunes of the desert. The hills surrounded the area, except for a flat plateau that eased into the water as if inviting a visitor. At that spot, the clear water lapped against the sand and gradually deepened as it joined the even deeper water that filled the gorge leading back to the river. Around the pool were tents placed on the tops of the low hills, which afforded a view of the pool. Those who had come more recently camped behind, so the area resembled a nomadic campsite.

I first saw the camp and pool as I came over a steep hill and stood at the top. The ground sloped gently down a long distance to the pool itself. I could see that John was in the water, and a small line of people waited in the shallows for their call to baptism as a much larger crowd of people watched the events from the lower hills. I realized I made a more dramatic figure than I wanted to as I stood on the top of the knoll, seeming almost to loom down on the group below, and my feelings of unease increased as I saw John look up toward me with the eyes of the crowd following his in slow unison. The meeting of our respective gazes had an almost palpable effect on me, as if some unseen hand had pushed me to alertness.

We stood immobile for what seemed a long time, with John's arms dropping to his sides and me leaning on my staff and staring across the distance, allowing the flow of sunlight, water, spirit, and thought to filter through my eyes and mind, until I knew what I must do. One step at a time, I began to walk down the hill toward him.

As I said, it was a long way, and it seemed that with each step, both focus and spirit increased, until the moment was pregnant with energy and intensity, with our eyes joining in more exact communion as I crossed the void to meet him.

I had never experienced exactly those sensations. My approach had become an event separate from the cohesive continuum of my life, as if in climbing to the top of a hill and looking out across to the new horizon, I had discovered a world completely different from the one I had known. I suppose that was pretty much what was happening. After shaking off the discomfort of suddenly finding myself the object of attention to such a crowd and realizing that the private familial meeting I had envisioned was not to be, I resigned myself to the circumstance, opening my heart and mind to God and asking for advice.

I had time to think. Each step held a thought, a question, or an answer. After I moved only a few paces, the vista before me became bright. I saw clearly the crowd of suddenly subdued onlookers blending in with the desert and the water, and I saw the flickering motion of their tents and banners. I saw John standing motionlessly in the shallow water with his long black hair and curling, chiseled beard framed with light from the sun and water. Other than the quiet ripples of movement from the tents, there was no motion or sound, only a fullness, and I knew with certainty—or felt with certainty, to be more correct—that all of us were sharing the same moment. We were like a crowd within a single tent, all rapt upon the same actions taking place before us, entirely caught in the enchantment of the extraordinary events that were unfolding.

My discomfort returned, and although I don't think I actually stopped walking, my mind certainly put a halt to what was going on. Why was so much attention on me? Was I playing the prince or perhaps the prophet? That felt like vanity and posturing. Why did it seem I could not stop, turn around, or simply take a place with the others on the shore? My life had been without fault, and I'd achieved that without effort due to my original nature's freedom from the irremovable dye of imperfection. Pride and the need to be admired had never held the slightest temptation, yet here it seemed I had engineered, consciously or subconsciously, an opportunity to hog the stage.

Answers came quickly even as my eyes dropped to the ground and then rose to meet the man who stood before me. This was it. The stories my mother had told me about John, my birth, and my birthright as the Son of God, ideas I had thought about at leisure and when it suited me, could no longer be shuffled off into the confines of memory to be ignored or pulled out for a few minutes of speculation. I had always known they were true, and I had almost secretly tried to make sure I lived up to whatever gift I had been given, but I had never tried with force of choice to bring those mysteries into greater prominence.

I had known for months that my life had to change. That was why my mother had said it was time to go see my cousin John. I remembered each word she had told me about him as clearly as I recalled everything that had been said about myself. Had it not become clear to me over the last year that if I was to believe in what had been said about me, I would have to believe in it all, even the hard part—that God was to give me the Throne of David, and I was to rule over all the world in God's name? Was not John to go forth with the spirit of Elijah to prepare the way? If all of that was really true, at some point, I was going to have to accept it and become it with my full devotion. It was dawning on me quickly that I was at that point. I also realized John had made this moment possible for me. He had started the whole thing rolling when, at God's command, he had irreversibly abandoned tradition and begun preaching to Israel to repent, return to God, and prepare itself, in fact, for me. At that moment, all of those formerly abstract notions became real. I was at the center of a vortex of energy, spiritual and human, and I had to decide to either drop all pretense of believing that the words said about me were true, turn around, and go back to Nazareth, content with my life as a carpenter, or accept it all, swallow my humility, and move on, accepting that I did indeed have a grand destiny.

I finished those thoughts as my eyes again met John's. I could see he had been thinking the same thoughts as I. He was remembering the same prophetic words that he had heard as a child. They had been repeated often as he grew up, and he had come to accept them in the full light of truth. He had moved ahead fearlessly with the will of God. Now there I was. I have never felt such love and gratitude for another man as I did at that instant. John's appearance was almost wild yet striking. He was a paradox of strength and mildness. It was easy to see why he had captured the interest of the nation. His gaze was calm and strong but filled with nuance, power, and a certain joy that played around the edge of humor, a word I had never heard used in relation to John. We had met as children several times but not since we were boys, and the image of the man I saw before me held little resemblance to the shy and withdrawn boy I remembered.

I had always liked John; even as a child, he had held a pure kind of resolve that I found reassuring, but we had never become close, as if we both had known it was not the time to compare our visions of the future. But now the time had come, and within those first few yards of my approach to the pool, we silently completed the discussion of our related lives. He knew who I was, and I knew who he was. He had allowed me to grow in power and knowledge in relative obscurity while he began the assault on the world. He had gone to Judah with the message that my arrival had come; the time had come to give up the expediencies of hypocrisy and weakness pervasive in the priesthood and the nation alike. It was time to remember God and all he had said, ask for forgiveness, and prepare for the approach of the Kingdom of Heaven.

But was I bringing that kingdom? I supposed it was possible, but that question I cast into the future, and with a new joy welling up within me, I left such thoughts and made my way toward John with new purpose.

It was as if the remaining twenty yards were the only path that existed. I sensed and saw, in a fashion just above human vision, a canopy of light, and behind that canopy, I knew, were angelic eyes.

By the time I reached John and clasped his arm, neither of us had words. Then he spoke words like the strong desert honey he ate: "I have need to be baptized by You, and do You come to me?" [2]

I stared at him for a moment before I realized that indeed, I did need to be baptized by him, for he had been given it as a sign of what was to occur, so I replied with as much kindness as I could, for I somehow knew we would have little time together, "Allow it now, for it is becoming to us to fulfill all righteousness." [3] I saw that he agreed, and I made my way up the bank to await my turn.

I turned back toward John when I reached a small dune just out of the reach of the water. The people had returned to themselves as my motion away from John broke the grip of the previous few minutes. They were looking to each other, mumbling words of conspiratorial amazement, and soon the few who had been awaiting baptism before my sudden intervention on the scene began to make their way to John, who spoke to them and led them in prayer before immersing them in the water. The baptism was not performed as a cleansing of their sins through his authority from God but as an act of repentance on their part, a request for a sense of right and wrong, and a sign of renewed devotion to their God. I could hear him speak to each one, and though I missed some words, I could tell each message was for that person alone, with the tone changing from sympathy to affection, from warning to encouragement. Each man received inspired advice, a clue as to how to live his new life. When John had finished his questioning, he would ask if the man wished to pray. Some did, but most let him lead them as they approached the heart of the universe to show dedication and renewed submission and to ask for reconciliation.

Many people made their way to John that afternoon, and the power of the events of the day decided many of the uncertain ones. As the last, a young woman, came out of the pool, I made my way into the water.

John's baptism was a baptism of repentance and a re-dedication to obeying the will of God by adherence to the Law of Moses. Since I had committed no crime under the law, I had nothing to repent, and I wondered why I felt compelled to do this thing. As I stopped before him, captivated once again by the power of his presence and surprised by the way the light of my own being rose to meet his, I began to pray. I addressed my God first by silence, until I found the thought that mirrored the truth of him. He was all things, the center, and living Creator of all things past and present. He was love and nothing else, capable of nothing but love. Then, by faith that thought had brought me close to God, I felt confident to proceed. "I do not know why I take this baptism, Father, but should I refuse to show my dedication to you in any way? No, I approach you in love and gratefulness, asking that you clarify why I am here and what I am to do. I know that you have blessed me, but of some things I am unclear. I ask that you give me knowledge so I may serve you according to your will."

The great hands of John gripped the sides of my head, and the power they held filled my head with a bright golden light. I felt myself being pulled backward as his thumb and finger held my nose against the water. The coolness of the water moved quickly up my back and arms until I felt my head immersed and the waters close over me.

God is everywhere.

I was holding that thought as I came up out of the water. God is everywhere. Did the water daze me? No, my mind felt sharp and alive, and indeed, I did agree that God was everywhere. The sky above was white, either by cloud or light or both, and I saw blue strips of day along the horizon against the gold of the desert. As I took a breath, I was awake, and my eyes returned to the sky.

The clouds broke in the center of the sky and began to fall toward me. Rigid billows edged with gold grew and curled toward me, gathering speed as if they were new light. When the pouring sky reached me, the force that I braced myself against never came. Instead, the clouds, the sky, the light, and the heavens themselves passed through me and into me. I was left alone in the center of a sphere that was the universe. The heavens and the earth were me. My senses were aligned with celestial motion occurring limitless distances away, yet they were my feelings within me. My size seemed limitless. I moved my arm to see if I still had form, and I watched and felt the arm move through space like a net through water, with ripples of force moving out and disappearing. I saw the effect of the motion of my arm, and I saw and felt the ripple of causation that moved out into the circle of the world. I saw with the dreamlike eye of my mind the rise and fall of the new alignment of the universe, changed because of one small action by my body. I saw caravans turn to face their homelands; women held their infants up above their heads, smiling up at the little faces above them, and men on horseback slowly turned their heads toward the east. Everything moved and then, as the moment passed, settled down like snowflakes to the still silence of my motionless present. God's Spirit had come upon me, and it remained with me.

On the earth, separated from God and heaven, experience and choice are small, and our ability to shape, share, and feel the environment around us is numbed by this separation. With the Spirit of God within me, I had no such separation. I shared creation with all. My will was the will of God.

By God's Spirit, I held the heavens within me, and since I was the stuff of earth, the kingdom of heaven had indeed come to the earth. Unlike the kingdoms of the earth, which maintained their dominion by force, what I was experiencing came from harmony and could not be put aside. Even the simple motion of my arm was uniquely in accord with the will of the Spirit, which monitors God's will. The billions upon billions of effects that the motion of my arm created passed through the universe like a breeze, joining the billions of other actions taking place at that moment.

The world around me was frozen. The crowd was asleep or in a trance of introspection, unable to understand what they had witnessed. John was looking down; the rush of Spirit had come to him as a vision in the form of a bird and then as the voice of God, which had said to him, "This is my beloved son, in whom I am well pleased." [4]

I thought before I moved, for I guessed, after viewing the tide of causation the motion of my arm had caused, that a turbulence would begin when I walked, and I thought it best to know beforehand how I should proceed.

Spirit spoke to me in a voice that was both words and a great flow of love, igniting the thoughts it conveyed into complete understanding: "Simply move; your path is before you."

I turned and made my way out of the pool. I was relieved to see my action had little effect on the world around me, for though I now walked in both heaven and earth, I had instantly decided, by request of Spirit, to exert no control over that world for the time being.

In the near distance, I saw the hills where I would head. The path led south along the Jordan. I was walking without thought. Spirit hurried me on with a gentle force that made my motions effortless and swift. I noticed the sun set, rise, and set again. The journey seemed to neither have nor take much time, and soon I was climbing up into the solitudes of the Judean desert. I suppose it was wilderness, but to me, it was like a low heaven for the grandeur of its tumbled stone and the mystery and fluidity of its sand. I saw the place where I was to sit: a smooth, hollowed alcove worn into the stone cliff by wind and sand that had long since blown another way. I sat against the cool wall of stone; my back and body seemed to melt into it until its reassuring strength described my position like a good chair. I was tired, and I closed my eyes to meet the darkness, which was still glittering with the sparkles of the desert sun but faded after a while to a thick, soft black that, if I'd looked, I'm sure would have held the images of quiet stars.

Chapter Five

When I awoke, indeed, the stars were out, bright, and perfect. I was instantly awake, although I did not move. My mind raced across the events of the day, and I closed my eyes. I was overwhelmed. What had happened? I tried to relax, grasping for perspective. I could feel I was still myself, and I began to calm down. I was myself, but I was far more. What had happened was not like anything I had expected. I mean, I knew that in God, all things were possible, but how could the universe have passed through me? Was nothing real? In meditation and prayer, I often felt God as a great center of light that enveloped me and gave me the feeling of an infinite, timeless love. But those moments were constructs of my mind seeing what it knew was there. What had happened to me happened to me; it was not a construct. The actual physical world had turned itself inside out, and it had left me no connection to anything that could be called real. I saw that God was absolutely without limits. God could not be limited to any one thing, for that thing had to exist in the context of other things to be defined. Those other things were also God. So there is only perception. God allows perception. Creation is perception. That seemed true, but what was I in the context of what I now knew?

My head felt compressed by the complexity of my thoughts, and I took a breath and relaxed again against the rock. I felt warmth and light above me and then in me. I was being shown something, being guided. Suddenly, I was immersed in a space so bright and heavy that I knew it was more than myself. It was eternity. It was God Itself. The sensation diminished to a level where I could imagine myself looking out over what I can only call everything. It was without shape. Light and what seemed to be sound or joy were all. It was increasing, and its increase seemed to go on and on, until it burst out of itself, and I saw what appeared as a new thing: a small sphere within the oneness that can only be described as conscious. Then I experienced blackness and the feeling of falling and gently coming to rest in silent darkness. As light began to slowly increase around me once again, the familiar voice of the Spirit began to inform me.

What I had seen was my own birth as the Son of God. Spirit continued to show me events. I was not experiencing now; I was being shown. I was shown eternities of time in which patterns emerged, disappeared, emerged again more clearly, and then almost disappeared again more quickly, until I felt as if a great flashing light was all there was. I was given knowledge—select bits of understanding that went back before beginning after beginning, creation after creation, universes, angels, communities for the creations, and complexities of glory—until I knew that what had been me had been there with God. I was the first creation, being with and then participating with God until the creation was abundant with spiritual beings and spiritual environments. Beauty, power, and love were among the things that were.

The act of creation continued. At one point, moved by God, Spirit separated a portion of itself into two. The illusion of darkness was introduced as the space between the two halves. The force of the separation was immense, and immediately it was clear that the nature of the fragments held an even greater force to reunite. God remained within each fragment as instruction on how to behave—not God himself but a blueprint for the energy to flow along. One fragment of each force joined together as a unit, complete with its inner spiral of instruction. Unable to resist the inertia of separation yet forced to acknowledge the even greater demand to reunite, they spun. Time was born. Time was the amount of spinning, uniting, separating, and transforming they would all need to do before they were reunited as One. With the help of Spirit, all of the limited fragments began an irresistible journey to that glorious return to the One they were. Along that journey, the earth was made.

First came starlight. Light is a signal of the objective, for light is the result of a portion of the separated Spirit being forced into union again by the play of the divided forces. It is life-giving because it is real and whole. In the process of light's creation, the individual units of one are also forced into union with each other, yielding the light but showing another tempo in the march to completion. The one becomes two, then three, then four, and so on.

The earth represents a further stage of this process, wherein a lot of time and energy is contained in the overall design of another path to the inevitable resolution: Life.

The earth is, of course, matter—ninety-two, say, bundles of united units, each with its own built-in instructions on how to behave. These properties result in an architectural journey between the elements that do not use heat and pressure to produce light but, rather, cooperation and interplay. Encouraged on by light, they move in the slow spiral of their design, proving and improving their intent over time. Eventually, there appears life. It's simple at first, a glimmer, as all creation begins, as I began.

Being locked in time and space, life has only one way to go: into the next moment. It grows larger and larger as it creates its own environment, its own atmosphere, and acts and reacts to the nonliving material and conditions around it. As it grows, it absorbs more and more of the material around it.

Life, like light, has already reached its goal. It is One again. But it does not abandon its unresolved partners in time-space, and it uses two methods to include them: it reproduces, and it reabsorbs. These fundamental processes allowed life on earth to prosper. But there are more aspects to united Spirit than life and light. As life began to take hold upon the earth, it began to show more aspects of its nature as a part of God. The beauty of the creation showed the sublime, irrepressible nature of the dual forces to reflect the perfection of God in their slow dance to where they began.

Life included consciousness in the animals upon the earth. But it was not self-conscious. Life, as with light, was perfect in its own right, but neither was equal to the full sum of the eternal, undivided worlds of heaven. There was another step to take for life.

God used the proceeds of the success of life as a bridge between the separated and the unified. He made Adam and Eve. Animal life had developed all the sophistication required to take a quantum leap. In Adam and Eve, he added a connection between life and the undivided, perfect, and eternal Spirit. Through reproduction and absorption, humanity could offer a conduit to the divine unity in a rich and beautiful way, displaying all the miraculous attributes of divine nature along the way. This is the purpose of all creation. This was the purpose of the earth.

Animal life was innocent. It relied upon millennium after millennium of experience to determine its actions. Each new life was unique, with its own genetic instructions, instructions subconsciously carried out by the perfect life that dwelled within the body. Choice was instinct. Adam and Eve had actual choice. They had instinct, but they learned from every instinctual choice they made. They were comprised of all their animal heritage. Man was made perfect in his archetypical appearance by the hands of God himself. In that final moment of creation, man was given the most precious gift of all: the potential to grow into becoming an eternal son of God— human. Hu, or son, is the word for the first male principal of God—both a being distinguished from God and a source of creativity.

God had made a garden for man, so when man drew his first breath, he was present in peacefulness and beauty that reflected his own.

When the work of fashioning the earth was complete, it was the seventh day, and God rested. All the angels who had assisted in the creation of the earth celebrated with God, and it was good.

Adam and Eve continued in the garden, being and learning. God had made only one rule for them: they were not to eat of the Tree of the Knowledge of Good and Bad, which was near the Tree of Life in the middle of the garden. They had no reason to eat of the Tree of Life, for they were young. God had promised they would die if they were to eat the fruit of the Tree of the Knowledge of Good and Bad. Adam and Eve were born with the innocent consciousness of the animals. There were no rules for the animals; every decision was predetermined by what had gone on before. No wrong existed. However, Adam and Eve possessed choice, as every immortal spiritual creature in creation does. God had intended that the new humans exist in a state of innocence for a time so they could learn if any of their instincts proved to create imperfect results not worthy of being taken into the perfect world of unity with God that awaited them— and of course, many choices would. The life existing in animals was far from complete, far from the high attributes that come with choice: compassion, honor, selflessness, and the bundle of wonderful qualities that make up love. With choice and innocence, they could improve themselves without blame. With experience in this self- refining, they would reach a point where God would introduce them to right and wrong, ceremoniously and actually, through the absorption of the fruit of the Tree of Knowledge and duality. They would then be equipped to ultimately travel seamlessly to the worlds of perfection. They, and their children, would possess the ability to face the challenge and joy ahead, transmuting matter into energy and love, living and creating ever more beautifully and intricately, until finally, eternally, they would be One again and slip from time and space into an ecstasy of union with Spirit and God.

One of the angels deeply involved in the final stages of the creation on earth disagreed with God on that point and told Eve so. He maintained that by eating the fruit, she would not die but would become just like God. Eve, and then Adam, ate the fruit. The angel knew God could not lie, but perhaps he felt he could bring humanity to perfection without God.

God and the angels who did not side against him left the earth. He closed off access to the Tree of Life. He did not abandon his authority—he cannot—but God ceased to guide the earth as an active creation of his own. However, God always maintained a direct connection to one man at all times upon the earth, and through one man, Jacob, God created a nation: Israel. Israel he would shepherd until the time of my life.

Man and the angels who remained would be left to pursue the path they had chosen, a path that began with a rejection of the only rule God had given the earth.

Once again, I saw myself as the Son of God. I felt myself agree to what God had asked of me, and then I felt awareness begin to fade and the feeling of falling embrace me with emptiness.

I fell for a long time; then there was nothing. Then came a stirring and then a glimmer, and I knew who I was. I was the baby Jesus. I had been shown what I had been and who I had become. The memory and wisdom of my life as the Son of God were gone. The glimmer of life that remained God had entrusted with the task of becoming a man and saving the earth from its current destiny: a plunge into the degradation and death that are the inevitable results of error. In the worlds of God, no error can ever become the beginning of something that lasts. This is not through conscious opposition but simply a mechanism of heaven. The emergence of error itself creates an unstoppable force that eliminates it.

But God did not create the world for nothing. I was to be the alternative.

I began to awaken as if from a trance, and in that awakening, I realized that the being responsible for man's need of rescue was standing near me. I suppose he wanted to make his case and see the depth of my resolve. From the moment Spirit joined me after the baptism, I became the center of creative energy on the earth. Satan pressed up against that new reality and was in opposition to it. He was with me every moment as I wandered into the mountains. He wanted to test me and bargain with me. He came as a quiet man— handsome even. He complimented me, saying I had done well. I was physically exhausted and hungry, and the world appeared more like a trance than what I remembered as reality, but as soon as I thought that thought, I noticed that all my faculties were intact, and I felt the presence of knowledge and Spirit and the return of clarity.

Satan suggested I should eat. I had the knowledge of all things physical and could simply transform a stone into food, he said, insinuating there was nothing wrong with that. Perhaps there wasn't, I thought, but the next thought was that if God wanted me to eat, he could surely do better than a stone. I pointed out that the scripture says man does not live by bread alone.

Satan grew angry with what I said, and I shuddered as a sudden force of noise and movement lifted me up from the ground. Then we stood together on a battlement of the temple. "Cast yourself off," he said. "No harm can come to you in your present state." I responded that the scripture warned against such tests of our Creator, thinking how pointless such an act would be.

Suddenly, life shifted, and I felt a great happiness within me. We stood high upon a mountain, looking down over a tranquil and serene earth. I felt the powers of love and strength pouring out of the lives below and saw their shrines, temples, and great works, which emanated pride and achievement brought about by hard work and care. It was a good place, and I was enchanted for a moment. I could see not just what was in front of me but also, somehow, the whole world laid out—cities, townships, and humble cottages in numbers bewildering to the eye. "This is all mine," he said. "Is it not grand?" Without waiting for an answer, he added, "This is mine. Acknowledge the greatness of what I have done as god of this world, and I will give it all to you, as to me."

I looked him in the eyes, and I will not say I felt pity, but perhaps I did. I said with all my heart, "Satan, you know it is only God who can give us happiness." There was silence, and he withdrew.

Chapter Six

I was alone with my back once again against the reassuring stone of the alcove. I took a deep breath, and with it came the realization of how hungry and weak I was. I had been away for forty days, or so it is written. I closed my eyes in prayer, and almost instantly, I was able to tap into the vast reservoir of spiritual strength and power I now possessed. Joy sprang upon me, and with the uplifting of my spirit came the sound of music and a sound I had not heard in thousands of years: the sound of the angels in flight. After a time, the sound became the tinkling of speech, and I saw the bright forms hovering about me. Out of courtesy, the many became few and took the more earthly form of winged maidens. They were radiant and beautiful and with substance enough that I could see the variations of color in their kind eyes and shades of complement in their long, billowing hair and white robes.

I was fed the pure water that is truth itself and the soft sweet bread of life that is incomparable to any food in the universe, filling my body with strength and willing energy. It was a moment of purity and love; gratitude on my part, of course; and a joy of such intensity that it struck the edges of the deep sorrow all spiritual creatures feel when they come close to the earth.

Within a short time, I realized I had to get up. I was anxious to return to the world and to be about whatever I was to be about. I was already walking before I had given any thought to my destination. I kept going and was soon where I wanted to be, as is the way with things when harmony is present. I found myself looking down upon a valley of unimaginable beauty that stretched to a distant horizon. I knew this was my destination.

As I walked, I went over what I knew. I knew clearly now that I had been born in perfection, and consequently, when I came into contact with God, when I became enlightened through Spirit, I stayed enlightened through Spirit. No other man could maintain that. The impact of enlightenment on most men is enough to make them stop and think about it, thus reopening the rift of error. I did not need to make such an error. I had perfect spirit in conjunction with perfect body. I was architecturally identical to Adam, except I had no intention of ignoring a rule given to me from God's mouth. I had no intention of disobeying God in any way, and God had so far given me no rules other than the law of Moses, which I was born into. If I did move toward doing something that would not harmonize with the will of God, then I knew I would be given warning. I knew the earth and its history, and I would accept no advice from anyone less than the Spirit of God or God himself without long and detailed debate. I had no need to make a mistake.

Within a short time, I realized I had to get up. I was anxious to return to the world and to be about whatever I was to be about. I was already walking before I had given any thought to my destination. I kept going and was soon where I wanted to be. I found myself looking down upon a valley of unimaginable beauty that stretched to a distant horizon. I knew this was my destination.

As I walked, I again went over what I knew. I knew clearly now that I had been born in perfection, and consequently, when I came into contact with

God, when I became enlightened through Spirit, I stayed enlightened through Spirit. No other man could maintain that. The impact of enlightenment on most men is enough to make them stop and think about it, thus reopening the rift of error. I did not need to make such an error. I had perfect spirit in conjunction with perfect body. I was architecturally identical to Adam, except I had no intention of ignoring a rule given to me from God's mouth. I had no intention of disobeying God in any way, and God had so far given me no rules other than the law of Moses, which I was born into. If I did move toward doing something that would not harmonize with the will of God, then I knew I would be given warning. I knew the earth and its history, and I would accept no advice from anyone less than the Spirit of God or God himself without long and detailed debate. I had no need to make a mistake.

In my life, I had often seen the world with such clarity and spiritual enthusiasm that the light of the higher worlds shone down onto the images of what I saw. That had diminished when I became more involved in the affairs of men but returned on occasions when I sought solitude and peace or when events went well for the Spirit and we rejoiced in a few moments of higher vision together. Now this vision was even clearer and tuned to the beauty of the earth.

It was breathtaking. It was early morning, and the sun was shining warmly on my face, illuminating the rough valley ahead, as I walked north and then east, back toward the river and the place to which I now knew I was headed: the camp of John, where my new life had begun.

I took my time walking back to the little oasis where John taught and baptized. I enjoyed myself and tried to think about what might be in the near future. Spirit had taken over my integration with the world, and though my being was still the operating center of the earth, it was no longer a conscious thing, and it seemed that in my normal movements of the day, there was no noticeable effect on the world around me. I experimented with that a little, fascinated that the Spirit could blend the massive spiritual force emanating from my being so seamlessly with my immediate environment that on the surface, I once again seemed like any other man. But the new spiritual center of the earth was having its effect on earthly reality. All things were moving according to their decisions based on the new information given them by their own spiritual awareness, although that awareness was for them, for the most part, subconscious. Even I did not see that great alignment taking place, for I had not thought to look closely at it in my meditation. I knew that what had to be would be, and it would be monitored and guided by the Spirit and by God. I also knew it would be well, and if I needed to pay special attention to anything, Spirit would give me a nudge or even speak to me to make sure I considered what must be considered.

I was interested in the way I had sunk so invisibly into the ordinary. I remembered my first few actions when the Spirit had entered me at the baptismal pond and all the cataclysmic and visual effects those motions had caused, and I remained amazed to see that had virtually disappeared. My experimentation showed I could still summon the immediacy of pure spiritual and physical power. The motion of my staff through the air could quickly attract force that became intense if I focused thought on the action for a purpose. I drew clouds from the far reaches of the desert and sent them scuttling on past my view. I formed them overhead so that they swirled around the vortex that the motion of my staff created. I even ignited the little storm I had created with a forceful thought that brought a clap of thunder and a sharp flash of brilliant light to the tip of my staff. After that, I had a moment's fear that I might have overstepped my purpose, and I dropped the stick and moved to a nearby rock to think. After only a few minutes of contemplation and a return to the serenity of the consciousness of God, I had a first long look at what I was about to do.

I knew that my people expected me, for I had studied with them in the temple and talked to them in their homes. It should be a joyous time, I thought, and I didn't look much further into the future, as I felt more interested in living the experience than examining it from above. I was excited. But there was something more to it, and as I searched for what I sensed, I traveled higher and higher into the worlds of heaven until I was near the throne of God. I did not see God, but from a place of great beauty that was once again the world, I heard my Father say, "It is I who have sent you here, and what I ask of you is to do my will. You are my Son, and you will not do other than my will, for I know you." As the words spread back to my earthly mind, I realized with clarity that God was explaining exactly what I had been thinking about earlier when trying to determine my boundaries and testing my thoughts and actions to see my limitations or lack of limitations. God had made it clear to me that I was to do nothing other than respond to events passively, and those reactions would be in accordance with his will, which would manifest itself in my natural responses guided by Spirit. I was to take no active role in correcting or disciplining the world. I saw that God's purpose for me was to allow the true nature of the world to reflect itself upon me. I was to let the world react to me, and again, what would be would be. Although I had the power to reshape the world in my image, for the time being, that was not what I was to do. I was to be obedient to God.

Speaking about God was something I wanted to do, so I got up and continued toward the oasis, but I did not hurry. My power and strength had not diminished; in fact, I felt a certain freedom with my new understanding of God's will, and I played for a few days, or perhaps weeks, with the desert, the sky, the breeze, and the scent of the desert flowers. In view of my new understanding of my role, I needed no instrument to concentrate my energy or attention or to lean upon for strength. It was a wonderful time, and even though the season was late, I felt no cold, and I suffered no hunger. I was like a bird playing in the whirlpools of the sky, enjoying the embrace of the wind and happy to see my food prepared when I grew tired.

But I was ready when I spied the camp ahead, and again, I felt excitement as I thought about seeing men for the first time since my baptism—or, as it turned out, my enlightenment. I walked around the camp and through to the nearest village, where I rented a clean, modest house for a few small coins. The house had a pleasant main room furnished with a strong table and several chairs. For the first time in months, I bought my own food and provisions and went to bed on a clean soft mat.

I awoke to a cool, bright day. I washed in leisure, enjoying the luxury, and retired to the front room to meditate and pray. Around noon, I made my way to John's camp. This time, I took the path that wound through the low hills dotted with a few trees, which were still green or green tinged with orange, as was the nature of the land at that time of year. As I approached the area where the pool began, a small stone wall edged the side of the path to my right, where the hill remained ascending and the path had been cut level to afford entrance to the area around the lagoon. As I was drawing close, I saw John look up and speak to the little group of men he was with. Although I was out of earshot for normal hearing, Spirit brought the words to me with clarity: "Behold the Lamb of God who takes away the sin of the world. This is He of whom I said, After me comes a Man who has been before me, for He preceded me." [5] The words filled me with appreciation. He indeed knew who I was and, leaving out things of little import, was telling those men that I had a prehuman existence. Although I do not think they understood, his words showed me again his directness and honesty.

I spoke to no one that day and retired early to my new little home. The next morning, I came again, and John was again there to notice my coming. That morning, he was talking to two men only, and my eyes immediately fell on them. They were striking, not simply for their physical appearance but also for the way they displayed a visible harmony with body, mind, and spirit. Again, John struck to the point as only the true seeker could: "Behold the Lamb of God!" [6]

As I continued on my way, the two men broke off from John and hurried after me. Seeing them follow me, I turned to them and asked what they were looking for.

"Where do you live?"[7] one asked.

"Come and see," [8] I answered.

So it began. John had given me everything to make it easy for me to approach the nation as a teacher, and now he gave me a gift in men: the first of my disciples, Andrew and John.

When we reached my house, we reclined on the divans the house supplied. I brought the thin wine I had purchased and offered them some of the good bread I had bought. We were all happy and excited, though I did not show it, and conversation went quickly and brightly, as it does when you find yourself with those with whom you have a lot to share.

The seeker who was a disciple of John and also called John was an imposing figure. He was fair for our people, with short, curly hair and bright light eyes not common to Jews. I was impressed with him—I think because my recent past had been so lofty in a way and so concentrated on the failings and futility of man that I was a bit surprised, and joyful, to see that a man could remain so pure and accurate in his thinking and perception as far into his life as John obviously had. He spoke of nothing but the Way, the sacred path that leads to God. Each word was spoken in order to bring back into the present moment the urgency and importance of finding truth and God. He spoke to teach, until you caught up, and then he would question you with open happiness to find out how deeply you shared his knowledge and vision. But his speech was never heavy or ponderous; each word was filled with light and a deep joy, as if he knew that what he was speaking would bring happiness. He knew the scriptures so well that they were woven into every thought, indiscernible from normal reason and logic but lending a power and authority to his words that made it hard not to believe what he was saying and want to learn more.

Andrew was different: small in stature and quick with action, word, and eye. Like John, he was handsome, and he had a confidence that made it easy for him to be the first to act and easy to accept that his action had been the right one. Only Peter, his brother, was quicker to thought and action and surer of his feelings. That was the way it would be with all my disciples— the twelve, I mean. They were gifts to me from God. They helped and supported me and talked for me. They relentlessly pushed me for answers, knowing, I suppose, that in time, they would learn the truth from me and thus, from God, their goal.

I referred earlier to my creative power going out into the world and invisibly realigning things to take into consideration my spiritual dominance of the planet. The disciples were as good a practical example of that as you can find. Now, when spirit aligns things on such a scale, time is not a factor. These men were chosen and prepared for me before they were born, although it was not manifest and brought into action in terms of present time until just a few months before. There was much they did not know, of course, and the kind of things I needed to teach them do not come from an afternoon seminar. They must be learned with the turning of the world. They must be taught by a mind and spirit that know what is to come upon the wheel of life and position themselves between the student and the moment to catch the meaning and illuminate it forever in the mind and soul of the student. This I could do.

Soon, satisfied with my answers, John asked me, "Who are you?"

"The Son of Man," I replied. A silence followed. They thanked me and left. Andrew did not try to contain his enthusiasm, and John left his happiness for a more careful meditation but felt awed, beginning to see the magnitude of what he thought might be true.

It was dark when they left, but it could only have been an hour before I heard voices at my door. There was Andrew, leading a man by the hand and saying, "This is he, Simon. This is the Messiah." I looked at the man who was being led so unceremoniously into my house. Simon was about the same height as John and also thin and fine looking. His hair was longer, and his lean face was shaped by an almost sharp intensity. Had it not been for the kindness of his eyes, I would have taken him for a warrior. He smiled, and a great blast of light came with his white teeth and bright, deep eyes. He stood and looked at me for a long time, and then his eyes dropped to the floor, displaying the great gentleness that lay beneath the energy of his personality. I almost had to laugh at the affection I felt for him, so pure and strong were the intelligence and warmth I saw behind the power of his aura.

He was a man who believed he was to be one with a great power, a universal power, and nothing smaller than the universe was going to stop him, but I could see that he knew somehow that universe was love. The power of my own being stopped him for the moment, though, and I could see that he accepted me at that instant, although his mind would have to understand that acceptance before he could be happy. "You shall be called Peter," [9] I said, because he was like a piece of the rock that is God.

There was nothing left to say that evening, but I told them I would see them in the morning.

I saw that John the baptizer and I were not to come together, and I did not question Spirit about it because I knew that it had to be. I did not want to bother him any more, for my presence kept him from work he had to do, and I did not want to make him sad in any way. That night, after the men had left, I saw in prayer that I should gather up my few things and proceed to Galilee. I was also told that along with Andrew, John, and Peter, three other men would accompany me. With that thought in mind, I cleaned the house and prepared to depart in the morning.

By the time I got to the camp in the morning, a small group of men were seated around a large fig tree not far from and just above the water. I noticed Peter there, and when he saw me, he began to approach. All but one man, who was in meditation under the tree, followed him toward me. I headed for a comfortable spot where we could sit and talk and reclined on one of the rough wooden benches assembled together for just such meetings. Soon the group approached, and I met them one by one. They were an impressive group. Even as I speak about it now, I become joyful in remembrance. They were beautiful men, each one individually the type of man one would remember and likely even comment on, but together they had such an effect, not just visually but also on all the higher senses, that I couldn't stop a smile from spreading across my face as I looked at them.

Peter's brother, Andrew, and two other men accompanied Peter. The first was introduced as James, the brother of John. James was unlike his brother, except perhaps for the quiet power they both possessed. James was tall, slim, and dark. His visage seemed to be carved from ebony, and he appeared to loom a little, not so much from his height but from the deep blackness of his eyes, which shone with intellect from beneath the angled brow and helmet of thick black hair. They were eyes you had to look at and from which there was no escape, so still, thoughtful, and silent were they. He was as quiet as his eyes, but when he did speak, those around him were silent for a moment while they considered the magnitude of what he said.

The other man was Philip, who was only slightly taller than James but heavier in girth. He had short-cropped hair and a short beard, and I think he, like I, was a bit overwhelmed with it all, translating the strong emotions he felt into a thin smile that was likely to erupt in great chuckles of laughter whenever something seemingly outrageous was said about the great things to come. The mere mention of the Messiah or the coming of the kingdom of God, not to mention following me as the Son of Man, was enough to bring a great fit of laughter from Philip. His head would rock up and down as his body rippled with happiness, amazement, and some justified uncertainty that his great, deep voice would soon verbalize. "You mean to tell me that God is bringing about the purification of the whole priesthood?" He would boom in amazement, looking to the side as if to get his bearings and then turning his head back to meet his partner in conversation with gleeful eyes. When Philip was not so engaged, he was slow and thoughtful, quiet, and content to simply go about his business. He volunteered little but watched and acted with strength and loyalty when needed.

The four of us talked for several hours. Philip brought food and wine around midday, and soon it was decided: they would go with me to Galilee. The decision was made simple for them by the fact that they all came from that area. That made it easier for them to come with me without confessing that they were fascinated and drawn by every word I said and by my person and that the true hope, almost too good to be true, was welling up inside their hearts. I was indeed the Teacher.

We adjourned to prepare for our journey, and I noticed Peter and James go to the man I had seen under the tree, who was now standing beside the water and talking to a group of Judeans. I watched as Peter spoke to the man, who looked toward me, obviously doubtful about what they were telling him. As they approached me, I said, "Behold an Israelite indeed in whom is no guile!" [10]

I said it so that they heard me, and as they grew close, the man, Nathaniel, asked me, "From where do You know me?" [11] I told him I had seen him under the tree, and I went on to tell him a little of what Spirit had shown me he was considering in his meditation. The accuracy of what I told him concerning his own thoughts astounded the man, and so certain was he of his own well-earned powers of discernment that he instantly said, "You are the Son of God. You are the King of Israel!" [12]

Nathaniel was tall and powerful. He was not heavy, but his body was of the nature of Taurus—so strong that his head was bent slightly forward from the pull of the muscles in his neck and torso. There was not a hint of humor in Nathaniel. He was serious and certain. The wickedness of the world was plain to him, and for some years now he had put away all triviality and focused his entire mind and strength on discovering and overcoming whatever had caused the world to be so without apparent purpose or justice.

In reply to his heartfelt faith in me, I responded to the whole small group, "I say to you, Hereafter you shall see Heaven open, and the angels of God ascending and descending upon the Son of Man." [13] That was enough for them, and we left that day for Galilee.

After crossing the Jordan, we headed north for Galilee. The weather was clear and beautiful; the worst of the cold season was seemingly over. The path was easy for the most part, and we took our time, enjoying the adventure of the journey and the fellowship growing between us. I paid attention to everything around us: the trees and the sand, the small red desert flowers that bloomed along the path, the wind and the sun, and the colors of the day, which shifted in golds, yellows, and mauves against the hills.

As I paid attention to those things, I made them a part of me; I extended my light out into the world with full consciousness—not enough to distort or change the natural world but enough to make it alive and under my will. I brought a brilliance and newness to our environment that the men could not help but notice. I was aware of every movement of every leaf and every cloud, every animal that stopped and peered at us as we passed, and every smell that the perfumed plants gave to the cool breezes to waft across our path. I made each moment a moment of awareness and awe so that my companions always had something to notice and discuss. I showed them, with the power of Spirit, the greatness of the universe and the majesty of that all but unspoiled corner of the creation. We were lifted—not above the physical world but into a deeper core of the physical world—by the power of my will. I did all of it with the full consent of God and Spirit, and it also taught me more about God's designs for my behavior on the earth. Of course, my friends were delighted, and the spiritual nature of the energy around them led them to conversations and reasonings on the nature of our world, our lives, and the deeper things of God. It was good. I felt no constraints upon my power, and I relaxed to an intuitive certainty that my will and the will of my Father were now in accord and that I could do, say, act, and exert power as I pleased, without fear that I would be in conflict with the limitations given to me.

That journey set a model for much of my remaining life. Other than the joy of giving the truth to interested men and women and seeing them understand and accept it, those were the happiest of times for both me and my disciples—enjoying the fellowship, love, and learning as we moved beneath the vast, open sky of God.

As we entered into the territory of Galilee, I was told, not without a fair amount of excitement, that in talking to a group of families traveling in our direction, Peter and Nathaniel had discovered that a wedding was taking place in Cana, Nathaniel's hometown, and my family was to be there. Peter told me we had also been invited—due, I suppose, to the interest being generated about me in the vicinity.

It was a large wedding, with family and friends coming from some distance to bring their blessings and joy to the bride and groom. For the Jews, weddings were the happiest of times, and there was great merriment around the house.

The feast itself was held outside in a large, walled courtyard with high white stone arches leading into a covered area where people reclined, talked, and sang. The arches were laden with a white climbing flower just in bloom; no doubt the wedding date had been set for the early blooming of that scented flower. Bright torches lit the walls, and light poured from the interior of the great stone house. Everyone was in his or her finery. As it was the cool time of year, that meant long tunics and bright sashes covered by thick, fine robes of every color. The clear, dark sky cheered the gathering on with its bright array of stars.

I was pleased to see my mother and my four brothers again, although beyond an embrace and several assurances that all was well with me, we discussed my life only a little. I think even my mother was a little hesitant to dampen the occasion with talk that could lead to concern or somber matters. My friends were enjoying themselves—rather cautiously, though. They wanted at once to tell everyone present about the stirring ideas they had been sharing and were anxious to talk about me and the events at the camp of John the baptizer, but they were hesitant to steal the attention away from the celebration.

Later in the evening, my mother came to me and, drawing me aside, told me that to the great dismay of the host, they were almost out of wine. At first, I dismissed what she had said, almost a little offended that she involved me in matters of a social nature, for that was not why I was at the wedding. But she persisted, asking some of the attendants to get me whatever I asked for. As it was, there were six stone jars nearby, a requirement for the purification rituals and common to many Jewish houses.

I checked myself, and Spirit moved with force. This was something I had to do. I told the men to fill the jugs with water. They did so to the brim. I closed my eyes for a moment, and when I opened them, a great feeling of happiness —even intoxication—came over me. It felt good that I could help those people; running out of wine would have ended the festivities on a sour note and brought despair to the bride and groom and their families. My heart opened in empathy. I instructed the servant to take some of the contents of the jugs to the man officiating the wedding and have him taste it. He exclaimed that he was surprised the host had kept the best wine for last.

My disciples—I call them that now, for after the miracle of the wine, whatever few doubts remained among those six were erased as far as the human mind can be free of doubt, and they were overjoyed and filled with new pride and certainty because of my display of power. As I mentioned before, I too was learning the boundaries of what God expected from me, and although there was no doubt that what occurred had been designed to occur, I had concerns about the triviality of the miracle itself. I experienced joy from being able to help and from being generous, but it was not yet my time to solve the small problems of mankind.

The next day was a day of rest for all. My mother and I met in the afternoon and had a meal together, during which she asked me all the questions she had wanted to ask me the day before. I assured her I was well and explained to her that my slightly cool response to her at the wedding had sprung not from lack of love or devotion but from the Truth. She took my fairly long recollection of what had happened since I left our home in stride, although she did break into tears, whether from joy, sorrow, or precognition I do not know— perhaps all three. Almost inaudibly, she spoke. "This is what has to be, Jesus, and I will pray for you every day. Never doubt that, but please, Son, be careful. You are my life itself." It was an emotional moment for me as well, with worldly feelings tearing at the heart as they gave way to greater ones.

Our conversation quickly changed to brighter things, and with a voice suddenly filled with more playful notes, she told me that she and my brothers would like to accompany us on the journey to Capernaum, where they were going in any event to spend some time with another cousin.

After another restful day and the reorganizing of our provisions, our somewhat larger group set out on the road to Capernaum.

Capernaum by the Lake, as some called it, was a beautiful place. Its well built white houses moved up from the Sea of Galilee to the hills and the plain above and further followed the roads that led off toward the world. It was an active place, with a fairly large Roman outpost and a tax office.

Many of the houses were modeled on Roman architecture, which I admit lent an added attribute to that already picturesque spot. Though it was a city, Capernaum afforded a certain isolation, for, as the town spread down to the sea, its inhabitants were virtually all Galileans, as they had been for centuries, and Galileans maintained their identity and their privacy. I knew Andrew and Peter lived in Capernaum, making their living as fishermen. James and John also lived nearby, just to the south, at a spot where the Sea of Galilee lay gently at the foot of a long, fertile plain. The sea was so clear and placid there that it was often called the Lake of Gennesaret after the lush green plain that rose above it.

When we arrived at Capernaum, I sent the men to visit their parents while I went about locating a place to stay, for I had known even as we approached the place that Capernaum would be the center of my efforts to reach the people of Israel. I was led by Spirit and my own inclination to a small white stone house not unlike the one I had occupied near the camp of John. It was to be my home, if home I had. I paid the owner of the house enough to secure it for what was to be the rest of my life. For me, it was a good place, deserving the name Capernaum, which held as one of its meanings "The Village of Comforting." My brothers spent some time with me, helping to make the house comfortable. It was suitable for an itinerant life but capable of holding quite a few people in relative comfort.

After the festivities at Cana, I wanted to reestablish a more appropriate mood for what lay ahead. It was not long before Andrew and Peter found my home, and the next day, the six friends and I took our midday meal together. After we had finished, I brought them together in silent prayer. Prompted by Spirit, I concentrated in prayer with the desire to bring us together in purpose. Almost immediately, the spiritual intensity of the moment increased, bringing bright light into the room, and with the light came a series of questions that we heard only as the silent voice of Spirit. The voice was not my own, but I recognized it as pure and allowed it to continue with the aid of my own mind and spirit, knowing the instruction that was to come was what I had requested and was sacred.

The questions were not unfamiliar to any of the men, but they were certainly not used to the way in which they were being addressed: by a force entirely internal. The voice was powerful and clear yet without any physical signs of sound or source other than the light that suffused the air around them. The questioning went on for some time; a thin synopsis would sound like: "What is it you are looking for? What is God's purpose for this world? How will his kingdom be restored to the world?" The answers came from the collective wisdom of their minds, prompted by Spirit if confusion or shyness kept the words from coming up within them, and they went something like this: "We are looking for the truth of God, to live perfectly in the perfect world of the loving Creator. God's purpose is that the earth be restored to its original state, perfect and timeless. His kingdom will come when he exerts his will upon the earth on his Great Day of Judgment. His rule shall be brought to the earth through the Son of Man, the Messiah." I encouraged the peace of truth to fill the room, feeling humble and a little surprised by the power of the event. The questioning stopped, replaced for a time by a tangible feeling of warmth and love. Such a thing never occurred again in my lifetime, but it forged a bond between us that lasted and remains.

Before we set out to Jerusalem to attend the approaching Passover, which was required of adult male Jews and was a law I would certainly observe as his Son, I needed the men to fully realize the importance and significance of my going there and to have faith in the truth of what I said and did. It is a difficult thing for a man to accept that the will of God has manifested itself in a human who appears just like himself. Even if the fact is accepted in the day, when the light is clear, such a thing has to be remembered and accepted all over again when one wakes up the next morning.

I knew one of my purposes was to tell the nation of Israel that God had responded to their prayers and prophecies by allowing a representative of his own will to come to the earth. That One had the promise of the ability to forgive the imperfection that caused death and the power to lead imperfect man through a transformation of the existing reality into the True Reality, a reality without death or pain and without end. I needed my disciples to truly understand that and know I was that person. The small miracle Spirit had performed in bringing us together for that first meeting in Capernaum gave me faith in them as much as they in me, and a part of me relaxed as I turned toward the future.

Chapter Seven

A week later, we once again took to the road, only this time, our destination was Jerusalem. It was hard for me to believe I had not returned to the temple since I was twelve years old. God had his reasons, I knew, and at the time, I was not inclined to search further for them, as the present fully occupied my attention. The mood was good. All along the path were the families of Israel, bright with enthusiasm over their own journeys, and of course, it was spring again. My disciples were happy and excited, almost like children, wondering, What will he do? What will he say? To be honest, I had no firm intentions other than to observe the Passover. Naturally, I knew I would do as I must. I was equally excited at the prospect of seeing the temple, and of course, I would teach.

As we walked into the outer courtyard, I had to stop. Instead of the sacredness increasing as we looked toward the inner temple, there was clatter. I observed makeshift stalls and the jumbled whine of haggling. Sheep and cattle were everywhere, and the money changers sat before huge bowls of coins, as if the purpose of the temple was to deal in profit. I knew that each worshipper was required to offer a sacrifice to the altar and that for the poor and many of the travelers hurriedly flooding into Jerusalem for Passover, it was sometimes difficult to find an offering or a money changer, but I also knew the temples of God had existed for centuries without the defilement I saw before me.

I felt no hesitation from Spirit; I took a multi-thonged rope from a man who was evidently a seller of cattle, methodically knocked over the first few stalls, and began to drive the sheep and cattle from the temple courtyard. "Take these things away from here," I told the sellers. "Do not make My Father's house a house of merchandise." [14]

Richly dressed men approached and asked, "What sign do you show us, since you do these things?" [15]

"Destroy this temple, and in three days I will rebuild it," [16] I replied calmly.

It was a hard thing for me to do, for I knew I made no friends that hour, at least among the Pharisees, who made a great profit from the selling, but it was a symbol of what was to come, and it was required of me.

I did not know what was expected of me or what I should do. My disciples and I continued with the preparations for the Passover meal, which began the next day at sunset. I had sent Andrew and Peter to find a room where we could celebrate the Passover and lodge for the next few days. They returned late in the afternoon, and by the time it was beginning to get dark, the seven of us headed down a series of winding stone streets toward our rooms. Since it was the evening before the feast, all Jerusalem was lit. Every house was bright, with light pouring out the windows of the thick stone walls that lined the streets and towered above us. Beautifully clad men and women were hurrying about, just as we were, making sure everything was ready for tomorrow. As on all Passovers, the moon would be full, so that night the great yellow orb hung above the city, as merry as the worshippers below. In all the history of man, there has never been anything as great as the people of Israel coming together for a festival before their God.

At dusk the next day, the Passover began with the evening meal. I reclined with my six friends before a great table set with velvet and adorned with silver goblets. Two great silver candle holders sat near the ends of the table, and large silver wine decanters held the sweet red wine we would pass between us, as was the recent tradition. I could not help but notice that the introduction of red wine to the ceremony, which was not required or even mentioned by Moses, must have been a silent prophecy in order that the Jews become acquainted with the wine that was to represent the blood of their Savior. My attention to that detail turned out to be intuition, for wine was used on my last Passover as a symbol of my blood and also as an obligation to remember. But I was not thinking of such things at the moment. I was enjoying the wonderful banquet my disciples had prepared.

It was so pleasing in every detail that I was surprised. The men were more enterprising than I had given them credit for. When the sun had set and everyone was clean, we informally positioned ourselves around the table and began our meal. Of the rituals, I will mention only one, the scriptural command: "When your sons shall say to you, What is this service to you?

Then you shall say, It is the sacrifice of Jehovah's passover, who passed over the houses of the sons of Israel in Egypt, when He struck the Egyptians and delivered our houses." [17]

It had been a difficult week. I was still upset over the incident at the temple, for the next day, I had a visitor, a Pharisee who'd stayed long and examined me with well-considered questions. He had expressed faith in me, but as I reviewed our conversation, I thought more deeply about what lay ahead, and I was disturbed. Soon my disciples could see that I was troubled, and finally, one of them simply asked, "Master, what is wrong?"

I looked long into his eyes and finally laughed. The evening was wonderful—was it I who would spoil it? We ate, drank, talked, and sang, as was the way. Later in the evening, when we were quiet and content, John said to me, "Really, Master, what is it?" I looked at him again and began to tell him.

I knew from my study of the scripture before my enlightenment that the Son of Man would not be well received. He would be crushed and carry the sickness of the world, and I knew then, from the vision of Spirit, that I must be sacrificed for the purpose of giving the world a new start. However, I hadn't expected that Israel might not recognize me—and by Israel, I mean the priesthood, which had always been the heart and soul of the nation, the ordained intermediary between the people and God. Would they actually not accept that I was the Messiah? I knew from experience who I was, and I had subconsciously thought that since it was true, God's representatives on earth would ultimately accept my status as the Son of God. But as of late, I had begun to be fully aware of what had always been there in the back of my mind: Israel might never fulfill its own prophecies and never experience the joy of receiving their Savior. I explained this to John, and he was stoic. "You are the Messiah, Master. Please be of good heart. The priests will do what they will do. They are so full of themselves they are blinded. God knows this and has taken it into account; it is his will we are working out."

We all talked about our future plans. The men were pleased they were being included in the decision-making. By midnight, we were in agreement that we would remain in Judea after the Passover and make a concerted effort to reach the Judeans with the message that the Messiah had arrived.

The six were determined we should baptize people in the fashion of John, as they were used to, and I agreed, although I myself would not baptize, for my baptism was to be of a different nature. The next day, we proceeded to the temple late in the morning. I was pleased to see that no sheep or cattle were being sold in the courtyard. My disciple Andrew, in fact, had heard on the street that many had long objected to that new and unscriptural practice but had done nothing about it until then, and they had taken the opportunity not to allow the livestock back into the temple, at least until further discussion.

We made our way through the court of women and into the court of Israel, where I had sat and talked many years before. I found a spot and began to pray, and my disciples did likewise. After they had finished their prayers, my disciples rose in unison, as we had arranged the night before, and set out to talk to the men of Israel. The basic approach we had agreed upon was that the men should ask all those who would listen first about John the baptizer and then about the One whom John had prophesied would come behind him. Did they know John had declared that the One had arrived? Did they know that One was the Son of God and the Redeemer of Israel? Had they heard of Jesus? Did they know I was in the temple? During all of that, I was to remain stationary.

At a prearranged moment, we all came together and walked from the inner court out into the courtyard. A considerable group of men followed us. The disciples approached those outside with the same discourse they had used within. After a while, as we had also decided the night before, John raised himself up to speak. John was a fine orator well versed in the scriptures and the law, and he spoke with brightness and intelligence that were contagious. Within a few minutes, hundreds of people were listening. Finally, he looked toward me and said, "This is he, the Son of Man."

At that point, I began to teach the listeners.

As I spoke, I opened my vision to the full brightness of Spirit in silent prayer. Soon there was a glow of light around me and around the disciples, who were standing near. The brightness grew until the temple building itself, just behind and above, began to glow with the pale, clear light associated with the presence of God. When I had finished speaking, the entire courtyard was silent in front of the illuminated temple. Without a word, we walked together out the temple gate, where our belongings had been brought for us. We continued through the busy streets and out into the countryside of Judea.

Our hearts were light but introspective as we came into the green countryside and the warm afternoon sun. We traveled later than usual that night, and in the morning, we walked until we came to a small body of water, beside which we made our camp. The following day, after a relaxed morning of food, prayer, and fellowship, the disciples made their way to the surrounding towns and roadways, approaching everyone they saw and speaking to all who would listen. My disciples had been the disciples of John the Baptist, and they were trained in bringing the attention of the local population to their teacher. With their new enthusiasm and knowledge of the events dawning over the land, they were now even more effective. Within a few days, there was a substantial crowd around our campsite, and I gave John and Peter permission to baptize as many as they could. After as many people as we thought were likely to come were baptized and advised of the arrival of the Son of God, we traveled on until we came to another likely spot with the availability of water suitable for baptism. We did this for nearly eight months.

On the Sabbath of the 240th day after we left Jerusalem, I received news that John the Baptist had been imprisoned by Herod. Three days later, we began our return to Galilee.

It was a long trip home. The weather was fickle and sometimes cold, not unlike many of the people we had encountered, but we were a satisfied group. We not only were close to each other but also felt we had done a difficult job well. One thing we were confident of was that Judea knew about us.

After a few days on the road, we were deep into Samaria, which was a barren, dry place in many areas, and we were tired. Since we had arrived near the town of Sychar, which was known to be the site of the well of Jacob, we sought out the well. I sent the disciples into the town to buy food but decided to remain and spend time in prayer and meditation beside the well that had been dug by the father of all Israel many centuries before. I had not been there long, when I noticed a woman approaching. As she lowered her bucket into the well, I spoke to her: "Give me a drink."

She was surprised but bold and said to me, "How do you, being a Jew, ask a drink of me, who am a woman of Samaria? For the Jews do not associate with Samaritans." [19] I looked at her, and I liked her. She was obviously intelligent and was fair looking despite the signs of a difficult life. I was prompted to speech.

"If you had known," I answered, "who it is that says to you, 'Give me a drink,' you would have asked him, and he would have given you living water." [20]

"Sir, you have no vessel, and the well is deep. From where then do you have that living water? Are you greater than our father Jacob, who gave us the well, and drank of it himself, and his children and his cattle?" [21]

"Whoever drinks of the water that I shall give him shall never thirst," I said. "But the water that I shall give him shall be in him a well of water springing up into everlasting life." [22]

"Sir, give me this water so that I may not thirst or come here to draw," she responded.

I said to her, "Go, call your husband and come here." [23]

I knew that she was sincere. Spirit instructed me to look at her deeply, and I saw much. "For you have had five husbands, and he whom you now have is not your husband." [24]

"Sir, I perceive you are a prophet," [25] the woman said in amazement. Revealing her spiritual interest, she added, "Our fathers worshipped in this mountain, and you say that in Jerusalem is the place where men ought to worship." [26]

"But the hour is coming," I said, "and now is when the true worshipers shall worship the Father in spirit and truth, for the Father seeks such to worship Him. God is a spirit, and they who worship Him must worship in spirit and in truth." [27]

She seemed genuinely impressed. "I know that the Messiah is coming, who is called Christ," she said. "When He has come, He will tell us all things."

"I Am the One speaking to you," [28] I told her, speaking as directly as I had spoken to anyone before.

When she noticed that my disciples were returning, she turned and went her way back to the town. I smiled, and when my friends arrived, I spoke to them, pointing to the town and the fields around it. I asked them to note that the fields were ripe for harvest and that already the reapers were in the field, collecting wages.

I did not simply mean the barley in the field, for it was a time before it would be ripe, but I spoke of the white color of the grain. I saw, and perhaps some of them saw as they looked where I pointed, the white color made by the Spirit working over the town and going to the minds of those who were receptive, making them aware of me. It was a welcome sign that our work had not been in vain and that a great harvest was being prepared, and even though the grain was not ripe in terms of the calendar, indeed, it was nearing the time, and our harvest would be one of men. The sign was a source of rejuvenation made even stronger when, within the hour, many of the men from the town came to us and asked us to remain with them for a few days. At the end of our stay, the men of the village openly confessed that I was the Savior of the world, and many of them truly believed.

When we reached Galilee a few days later, I sent the men to their homes. I stayed in the hills and thought and prayed, rebuilding my strength and sharpening my focus on what needed to be done.

When I was full of Spirit, I turned toward Cana, where I stayed until the man Spirit had told me to expect arrived. The man was an official of King Herod Antipas, and he lived in Capernaum. He had heard I had returned from Judea into Galilee, and he had rushed to me for help, for his son was sick. When I saw him, I barely listened to him before saying, "Return to your home, for your son is healed." [29] On the way home, he got word that his son had recovered at the very hour I had spoken to him. The next day, I left for my own village of Nazareth.

Foresight is a thing we all know a little about, and I don't want to elaborate on that too much here, but I can tell you that I was a little nervous about going back to Nazareth. I suspect the feeling of unease had as much to do with what I had already come to learn about men, especially religious men who felt they had a special status bestowed by God, as any hints given me by Spirit. But I tried to be positive. I showed up at the synagogue on the Sabbath, as I had every Sabbath before my departure to the Jordan River. The congregation was excited; it was obvious word had reached Nazareth that I had come home. We all greeted each other in a friendly manner, and when the service began, the overseer asked me to read, as I had often been asked to do, especially after my father, Joseph, died. He handed me the scroll of the prophet Isaiah, and the Spirit came into play as I noticed the illumination of a passage I knew well. I read,

> The Spirit of the Lord Jehovah is on Me;
> because Jehovah has anointed Me to preach the Gospel to the poor; He has sent Me to bind up the broken-hearted, to proclaim liberty to the captives,
> and the opening of the prison to those who are bound;
> to preach the acceptable year of Jehovah and the day of vengeance of our God;
> to comfort all who mourn;
> to appoint to those who mourn in Zion
> to give to them beauty for ashes, the oil of joy for mourning
> the mantle of praise for the spirit of heaviness;
> so that they might be called trees of righteousness, the planting of Jehovah, that He might be glorified. And they will build the old wastes,
> they will raise up the ruins of former times.
> And they will repair the waste cities, the ruins of many generations. (Isaiah 61:1–4 MKJV)

I stopped reading and spoke. I explained that to Israel was to come One who was anointed, chosen by God to restore Israel not only to the glory it had while David and Solomon ruled but also to a glory of which that rulership was but a symbol. The house of David was to establish true justice on the earth in God's name, not simply for a few generations but for all time, and the desolation referred to in the scripture meant not simply Israel's defeat at the hands of an earthly army but the fallen state common to mankind that had brought death upon us all. Then I said, "Today is the fulfillment of this scripture." [30]

It seemed to please the congregation, but within minutes of the end of the service, I felt the machinations begin. Some said, "This is the son of Joseph, is it not?" [31] with no feeling of affection but as an expression of doubt that I should, or could, aspire to such heights. If I was truly such a man, would I not have performed great deeds and said great things when I was among them? Most of the talk came from men who valued their positions in the congregation and were used to accepting all the praise that came their way. It was not seemly to them that I should claim spiritual greatness without coming to them to receive permission; bestow thanks on them; or, even better, perform miracles as payment for all their priceless spiritual guidance.

They never considered that the things they taught me they were obliged to teach, just as someone had taught them without need for reward. It took only a portion of an hour for many of the older men to reason in such a way and take that position.

When I pointed out scripturally that during the drought, Elijah was sent not to a widow of the women of Israel but to a native of Sidon, and such was the mystery of God's will, they became angry. I was astounded at their reaction. I had anxiety about coming home, but I'd never expected what happened: they rushed upon me and took me outside to a high cliff, where they tried to throw me off. I was never in any danger, for I knew Spirit had no intention of letting them kill me, but I had to exert myself and dull their senses in order to avoid just that. It proved to me, though, just how tight a hold Satan had on men of authority and how they had no real power of reason if he called upon them with true intent, for I knew he was about.

After my escape, I again took some solitude. I was relieved, in a way, that my visit home was over and a little surprised that my intuition had been correct but had underestimated the violence of what happened. But now I felt free. I could think of no further ties to the earth that needed to be unraveled, and I felt comfort in the fact that my disciples were men I could rely on to help and to learn. The next morning, I turned back toward what was now my earthly home: Capernaum. I was ready to begin my work in earnest, just as someone who has tried out the full circuit of a track returns to the beginning to see how well it could be run with full effort.

I soon found Andrew, Peter, John, and James at their boats in Capernaum. I was feeling strong and enthusiastic, and I wanted no hesitation from the men to match my zeal, so as you probably know, I urged Spirit to give the men enough fish to keep John's father, who owned the business, happy for a long time, although I knew he was a righteous man who would expect or require no such gift. As I had already set up the house in Capernaum, I asked them to join me, and we began preaching immediately. I had filled them with light as I had the fishing nets with fish, but that was hardly necessary because it was I who would take the lead in letting the nation know that the kingdom of heaven had indeed drawn near.

The next Sabbath, we attended the large synagogue in Capernaum. I did not hesitate to begin teaching the congregation, and I left no room for the kind of criticism I'd encountered at Nazareth. However, opposition came from a different quarter. On that Sabbath, a demonized man was present. After a while, he shouted with a loud voice, "What do you want with us, Jesus of Nazareth? Have you come to destroy us? I know who you are—the Holy One of God!" [32] The demon controlling the man was one of Satan's angels.

Rebuking the demon, I said, "Be quiet, come out of him!" [33] The demon threw the man into a convulsion and yelled at the top of its voice, but it came out of the man without hurting him. Even my disciples saw a new authority to my teaching.

After the service, Peter rushed to me, obviously distressed. His mother in law was gravely ill. We all proceeded to Peter's house, where I saw that she was indeed sick. I took her hand, and Spirit healed her instantly. She got up enthusiastically and felt so refreshed that she wanted to show me her appreciation by preparing us all an evening meal. By the time we had eaten, it was dark, and while the lamps were being lit, we saw a large crowd outside. To our surprise, there were hundreds surrounding the house, for word had traveled quickly about the healing of the possessed man, and the whole town was aroused. I went outside with the four and began to heal the sick.

I do not know how many were cured of their disease, but it was many. Some of the people were possessed of demons, and I ordered them out. As they left, they called out, "You are the son of God,"[34] I did not let them speak further.

It was late when I arrived home, but I could not sleep, because of the force of Spirit generated by all that had occurred. I got up before dawn and walked down to the beach, to an isolated place, to pray to my Father. Before the sun rose, Peter and the others found me, and Peter came to me to tell me that all the people of the town were looking for me because they wanted me to stay with them. I had the disciples sit with me for a while, and I explained that I must go to the other towns and cities around us, for I had come to earth not to enjoy the company of a friendly village but to teach as many as I could. They understood and assured me they wanted to join me wherever I wished to go. When we returned to Capernaum, the people besought us to stay, but my disciples helped to explain why we must go, and soon the crowd dispersed in a good mood.

For the next few months, we taught across Galilee, and many came to believe. The spirit healed, without partiality, the sick and infirm wherever we went. Soon it was not possible for me to stay in a town or city, because the throngs would become too much. Instead, I found the high and lonely places and slept there, usually allowing my disciples to stay with friends in town, although Peter and John often chose to remain with me. In the mornings, I went into the towns to talk and heal, and usually, I would withdraw before dusk. On occasion, we would take a meal at someone's home as guests; Andrew and Peter were adept at deciding who was trustworthy so we could relax for a short time in the comfort of a house without causing too much of a disturbance. People were searching us out from all parts of the country—from Judea and across the Jordan, from Perea and Decapolis, and even from as far away as Syria. On occasion, we slipped away and took a boat back to Capernaum. Once again, Peter and Andrew showed initiative by obtaining the use of a sturdy boat, and of course, all four were experienced sailors. When we arrived at Capernaum, it was usually not long before the people discovered our presence, and crowds would quickly assemble to listen, be healed, or simply watch.

On one occasion, I went to the beach and spent the morning talking to the crowds who had followed me out of Capernaum. As I was on my way back to town, I passed by the tax office. The tax collector was sitting in a small booth outside the building, as the weather had become warm again, and he looked at me as I was passing by. I could see that he knew who I was, and his large black eyes became soft as he looked at me. Through Spirit, we exchanged thoughts, and without hesitation, I walked to where he was sitting and said to him, "Be my follower." [35]

Equally without hesitation, he stood up and entered the building behind him. A minute later, he came outside and stood in front of me. "I have turned in my position as a tax collector," he said. "I will follow you."

Matthew was a large man. Although he was not tall, his body was massive and powerful; his thick neck was a seamless continuation of his jaw as his head joined a chest and stomach as round as the girth of two men. He was as strong as any man I had met, yet his eyes were those of a great calf, gentle and tinged with melancholy. He was strong of body but gentle and mild of heart, with a deep understanding of scripture that came from unusual effort and stamina at study, and most importantly, he knew God and placed that knowledge above all else.

We continued on together to the house, where I left him on his own to meet the disciples. That night, Andrew informed me, we were to dine at Matthew's house.

It was a lavish gathering. Matthew had invited as many friends as would come, and the majority of the men were tax collectors or other officials, for the people in general disliked such men or any man who dealt with Rome and, as a rule, would not associate with them. It was a wonderful meal, with luxuries we were not used to or inclined to, but it gave us an opportunity to discuss the truth with men and women whom it was difficult to be close to under normal circumstances. At the end of the meal, all of us were aglow with the pleasures of food and drink, and I thanked Matthew for the reception and smilingly but seriously said to him, "There will be few such meals as this from tomorrow on, Matthew, is that well with you?"

He looked down for a moment and then said to me, his great brown eyes moist with sincerity, "This world is only dust for me if I cannot please the Living God; I will follow where you go." From that day forth, Matthew was with us until the end.

Time had passed, and the Passover was again approaching, so we began making preparations to leave for Jerusalem. As we were doing so, three disciples of John the Baptist came to us. After they had eaten and felt rested, one asked me, "Why is it that we and the Pharisees practice fasting, but your disciples do not fast?" [36]

In answer, I said to them, "How can the guests of the bridegroom mourn while he is with them? The time will come when the bridegroom will be taken from them; then they will fast." [37]

I saw that the question, like most, had many levels. On one level, they knew that many of John's disciples had come to follow me, and it was natural for them to be upset by that, for it made them wonder if what they believed was true, so they wanted to see if they could find flaws in my teaching. Also, they were worried about John, as he had been imprisoned for some months now, and they were trying to see if we knew what might become of him. Added to that, they wondered why we would not at least fast while John was imprisoned. Did we not care?

My answer was fair, as it was John himself who had referred to me as the bridegroom, so they would understand the reference. But by my answer, I also wanted to allude to my death so that they might think about my words later and believe. I went on to say, "No one sews a patch of unshrunk cloth on an old garment, for the patch will pull away from the garment, making the tear worse. Neither do men pour new wine into old wineskins. If they do, the skins will burst, the wine will run out and the wineskins will be ruined. No, they pour new wine into new wineskins, and both are preserved." [38]

I said this for two reasons. First, I wanted to explain that my teaching was fundamentally new, and its conclusion would be the fulfillment and, thus, cessation of the written law, the cornerstone of Judaism. The teachings coming out of my ministry would not be a patched-up form of Judaism but an entirely new level of awareness of God. Also, I wanted that saying available in scripture, for it would explain to men in the future that in the last days, the world must realize that no institutions, structures of thought, codes of conduct, or even physical understanding of the nature of life itself would be carried into the new world. The new world would be just that: a new beginning for man; born into a new Heaven and a new Earth, and in that world would be The Spirit of God, glorious, sustaining, permanent. A world of unknowable mystery and energy that spoke of an unfolding future that will entice us forward, accompanied by the presence of a gentle teacher who will explain and reveal the infinite path before us.

A few days later, we left for Jerusalem. We left well before the Passover so we could stop in the towns of Judea and preach in the synagogues along the way. Things went well, but as we came to Jerusalem, an event occurred that became the theme for my undoing. There was a pool near the sheep gate of the city that was believed to have healing properties. It was the Sabbath when we passed by the pool, which was called Bethesda, and I was called to a man who had been sick for a long time. He was so weak that he was unable to lower himself into the pool at the appropriate time, (the waters would show agitation when the healing properties were present) as the others would push him out of the way in their haste to get in. I cured the man and instructed him to take up his cot and leave the place. As he was leaving, the Pharisees reprimanded the man for carrying his cot on the Sabbath. Later, when he learned that it was I who had healed him, he went to the Pharisees and told them it was Jesus who had instructed him to carry his bed.

On the day after the Passover meal, we were at the temple, and a large group of Pharisees approached me. When they had determined it was I who had healed the man by the pool, they began to reproach me. I thought that perhaps they would inquire as to how I had cured the man and come to see that I did such things through the Spirit of God, but no, they became even more hostile. Since we were at the temple, I did not want their base and unfounded anger to go unanswered, and I gave them a thorough response. As I said earlier in my story, I am not going to talk about every scripture that is written about me, but this one sums up many things and illustrates well the obstacle I encountered with the priests of Judah, which eventually became insurmountable. I am making a special point of this interchange because these were the things I had been so troubled about on the previous Passover and had spoken to John about, namely that I was beginning to have real concern that the Judeans would perhaps never accept me, and in my response to that new assault, I wanted to make an attempt to show them how important it was that they understand I was not a threat to them but was a part of their own faith.

In my response to the Pharisees' accusations that I had healed on the Sabbath and ordered the man to carry his cot, the record is this: I said to them, "My Father is always at his work to this very day, and I, too, am working." For that reason, the Jews tried all the harder to kill me; not only was I breaking the Sabbath, but I was even calling God my own Father, making myself equal with God. To that, I answered them, "I tell you the truth, the Son can do nothing by himself; he can do only what he sees his Father doing, because whatever the Father does the Son also does" (John 5:17–19 NIV).

I said those words because I had been aware since shortly after I came out of the wilderness that although I had the power to do things issuing from my own will, God had commanded me to do things only as I was directed by Spirit while I was on the earth, which would reflect the will of God.

I went on to explain, "For just as the Father raises the dead and gives them life, even so the Son gives life to whom he is pleased to give it. Moreover, the Father judges no one, but has entrusted all judgment to the Son, that all may honor the Son just as they honor the Father. He who does not honor the Son does not honor the Father, who sent him. I tell you the truth, whoever hears my word and believes him who sent me has eternal life and will not be condemned; he has crossed over from death to life" (John 5:21–24 NIV).

While on the earth, despite the fact that I would only do things as directed by Spirit, which were the will of God, I could accept the people who listened to me and believed, and through that acceptance, they would be offered the water of life, which was mine to give, as I had told the woman at the well.

I said, "I tell you the truth, a time is coming and has now come when the dead will hear the voice of the Son of God and those who hear will live. For as the Father has life in himself, so he has granted the Son to have life in himself. And he has given him authority to judge because he is the Son of Man. Do not be amazed at this, for a time is coming when all who are in their graves will hear his voice and come out—those who have done good will rise to live, and those who have done evil will rise to be condemned. By myself I can do nothing; I judge only as I hear, and my judgment is just, for I seek not to please myself but him who sent me" (John 5:25–30 NIV).

I talked about the fact that I would have a life and a will after my earthly course was complete and that then, when the new world was ushered in, I would judge those who would have life and those who would not, but even then, my will was the will of my Father. I wanted that out in the open, for the Sadducees were not really acquainted with what I taught, and they did not believe in the resurrection, so I thought it better for them to know that now than for it to be a thorn later.

I told them, "If I testify about myself, my testimony is not valid. There is another who testifies in my favor, and I know that his testimony about me is valid. You have sent to John and he has testified to the truth. Not that I accept human testimony; but I mention it that you may be saved. John was a lamp that burned and gave light, and you chose for a time to enjoy his light" (John 5:31–35 NIV).

As you know, I had great affection for John the Baptist and appreciated the fact that he accepted me as what I was with a full witness. The Pharisees had recognized John to some extent, and he had told them about me, yet they would not listen to him.

I said, "I have witness weightier than that of John. For the very work that the Father has given me to finish, and which I am doing, testifies that the Father has sent me. And the Father who sent me has himself testified concerning me. You have never heard his voice nor seen his form, nor does his word dwell in you, for you do not believe the one he sent" (John 5:36– 38 NIV).

I went on to remind them that even above the testimony of John, they should be able to recognize me by the great things the Spirit was doing through me. They could not accomplish the things I could, yet they would not believe.

"You diligently study the Scriptures because you think that by them you possess eternal life. These are the Scriptures that testify about me, yet you refuse to come to me to have life. I do not accept praise from men, but I know you. I know that you do not have the love of God in your hearts. I have come in my Father's name, and you do not accept me; but if someone else comes in his own name, you will accept him. How can you believe if you accept praise from another, yet make no effort to obtain the praise that comes from the only God? But do not think I will accuse you before the Father. Your accuser is Moses, on whom your hopes are set. If you believed Moses, you would believe me, for he wrote about me. But since you do not believe what he wrote, how are you going to believe what I say?" (John 5:39–47 NIV).

I expressed my frustration with them, for they claimed to be the teachers of the Word of God, and indeed, they were learned in the holy scriptures, but they seemed to pay no attention to them. If a Pharisee they did not know visited them from another town, they would give him respect and listen carefully to what he said, yet they would not even consider what I said, despite the fact that scripturally, they knew a Messiah was soon to come from God, one worthy of great glory and respect. Finally, I warned them that if they truly claimed to believe the Bible, the very words of Moses would condemn them.

All that I said to them only increased their opposition, and they became firm in their intention to kill me. Within a few days, we left once again for Galilee.

As it was the time of Passover, it was full springtime in Judea, and we were happy to be under the great blue sky, observing the rush of growth in the countryside. However, our joy was short-lived. As we were walking, the disciples grew hungry, and in the spirit of the moment, they picked a few heads of grain and, after rubbing them in their hands to remove the chaff, nibbled on them as we walked. It was not long before an angry group of Pharisees approached us. "Look, your disciples are doing what is unlawful on the Sabbath," [39] they cried out. I answered them, but I will not go into detail;

I think you get the idea.

Controversy over the Sabbath, the sacred day given to men as a time to appreciate all God had provided for them, a time for joy and fair thought, continued to grow as the excuse for my persecution. I suppose that in fairness, I should point out that on the Sabbath, we had the majority of our contact with the religious rulers, for we always attended the synagogues on that day, but nonetheless, the irony was strong.

On another Sabbath, we attended a large synagogue near the Sea of Galilee, having made our way up from Jerusalem while approaching our home. In the congregation was a man with a withered right hand. Watching closely, the Pharisees finally could contain themselves no longer, and one asked me,

"Is it lawful to cure on the Sabbath?" [40] Now they were comparing the miracles I had performed through Spirit to the normal practice of medicine, which people, by tradition, did not do on the Sabbath unless the situation was life-threatening. The tradition was taken to the extreme that a sprain or a broken bone could not be bound or set on the Sabbath. The man looked at me, and I asked him to stand up before the congregation.

"If any of you has a sheep and it falls into a pit on the Sabbath, will you not take hold of it and lift it out?" [41] I asked them. There was an answer correctly given that the scriptures said a good man was caring for the lives of his animals, so I continued. "How much more valuable is a man than a sheep! Therefore it is lawful to do good on the Sabbath." [42] No one answered, and I said to the man, "Stretch out your hand." [43] He stretched it out, and the hand was healed. Now, there was in attendance that day a Sadducee, one of the elite group of Jews most closely associated with the priesthood, who was also a member of the court of King Herod. Immediately after the services, he went to the political body of the court of Herod, and there they conspired to kill me.

The next day, Peter brought me word that the Sadducees and the

Pharisees were united against me, and they had joined with officials of the state to kill me, for every man in Galilee knew about me, and it was not possible for them to keep such a secret. Upon hearing that, we left for Capernaum, although we did not go directly to my home, for we did not want them to find us while they were still full of enthusiasm for my death.

After a time, we returned to teaching, and great crowds came from all the country around to hear me speak. Many of the people believed, and the four had been teaching those who were sincere, so there was a band of hundreds of followers who remained in Capernaum constantly. Nathaniel and Philip had joined us, and they helped with the organization and education of the many who considered themselves my followers. Most of them had some sense of my message and purpose and who I was, and of those, most had knowledge of the scripture and of the Living God who had created the earth and chosen us as his people. The six disciples trained those who did not have knowledge of the written law, or we assigned someone well versed in the truth to teach them. All were instructed in meditation, prayer, and the reasoning that went with the knowledge that the kingdom of the heavens had drawn near. The enthusiasm and happiness of the crowds was contagious. They felt saved in a way they never had experienced, or even expected, for Spirit had filled their hearts and minds.

Soon the crowds had grown so large that I asked Andrew to find boats for our use, so I could teach at the lakeshore, a few yards out into the water. That prevented the people from crushing ahead in trying to get closer to me, and also, it was good near the water's edge; the sky, sand, and water created a natural theater where I could easily be heard, for the weather was fine. With the boats, we moved from spot to spot up and down the coast and reached many, and we were able to satisfy the need to hear for all those who sought to listen.

My four great fishermen did indeed become fishers of men. Even I had not known in the months before, when I said those words to Peter, that the prophecy would have such a literal fulfillment. I could not have reached so many people in such a pleasant and successful way had it not been for the great skill with which the men handled the boats. Peter often stood behind me, overseeing the gentle rowing and paddling required to keep the proper distance and position from the shore. Both he and John were always there, standing tirelessly, their faces shining with spirit and appreciation not only for my powerful words, which came directly from the Spirit of God, but also for the men and women who listened. They watched the faces of the crowd, seeing the dawn of hope and happiness that came over those the Spirit touched, and remembered to seek them out later to help continue their movement toward the Way.

It had been about a year and a half since my baptism, and I came upon a time of reflection. I withdrew into a mountain close to Capernaum, a place we often sought out to relax and talk because of its beauty and comfortable glades. I walked to the top, where I sat under the stars of heaven and prayed and thought until the dawn.

With the increased hostility of the Pharisees and their new alignment with the State of Rome, I began to see—and Spirit did not deny it—that I did not have much time remaining. I considered what had occurred and what lay ahead. I saw that my life had fallen into two portions. One was the teaching of the people, and the other was reaching out to the ordained ministers of God, his priesthood. In Israel, priests officially represented God to the people. They did not take that task upon themselves but were given that responsibility by God. After they came out of Egypt, the Living God gave the sons of Aaron, from the tribe of Levi, the sacred duty of acting as God's agents to the people of Israel. Even as I walked the earth, there was not a priest of Israel who was not a son of the sons of Aaron. My Father had ordained those priests, and I could not put them aside. While I was pleased with the success my ministry was having with the people of Israel, I would not be legitimately accepted by the nation unless the priesthood accepted me—

and those very men, or the agents of those men, had designed to kill me. I felt a great sorrow over that. I was filled with love but was forced to accept the truth that many hated me and wanted to kill me. I was overwhelmed with sadness, and tears came. I shook off the feeling, but for the rest of my life, I could feel it—a deep heaviness that came with life on earth.

I knew what the priests wanted. They wanted me to give a great sign that would signify that I was restoring God's kingdom, and that being the case, they could look forward to becoming the priests to a nation that would for all time rule the world with the power of God. But that I could not do, for it was not God's will that the old wineskin of the earth be patched up to receive the new wine of eternal life.

However, neither was it God's will that they reject me. In God's name, John called out to them, "Repent for the kingdom of heaven is near." [44] The priests were entitled to hear the words of John and repent, for God had by no means taken that choice from them either by will or prophecy, but I saw that Satan had taken hold of those men just as he had the priests of the great temple of Solomon before it was destroyed.

So despite my pleasure at the fact that the masses were listening to me and being uplifted, that joy was badly marred by my knowledge that whatever gains I made with the people would be undone if the priests succeeded in triumphing over me, for make no mistake, the crowds who came to me were not free, as they appeared to be; they were on a leash forged by Satan through the priests. The leash was made of chain and blood, and when the leash was tightened, it could not be resisted without great power. As went the priests, so went the nation.

But I could abandon neither path. I would teach the people, and I would impart to them the glory of the good news: they would inherit the earth, though at present they were oppressed and downtrodden. For those who desired good, their suffering would lead to eternal happiness. I would not give up the nation; I would reason with the men of power until I had no breath.

As I was thinking those thoughts, the sun covered the green land before me with all the colors of the glory of the dawn, and I rose up and went down the mountain with the intention of organizing what I had so that all things might be accomplished.

When I reached Capernaum, I called to me the closest of my followers, and there were about seventy. Of them, I chose twelve to be the inner circle of my disciples. I had chosen them in prayer the night before, and they became known as apostles.

I chose Peter, Andrew, James, John, Philip, Nathaniel, and Matthew, whom you know, and I chose Thaddeus, Judas, Simon, Thomas, and James.

Thaddeus was a great man, and in another time, perhaps he could have been a king. He was of a height that seemed correct for a man and was strongly built but not heavy. His olive skin and greenish eyes were framed by shoulder-length brown hair and a short beard, which he allowed to grow longer under his mouth. He had great power and stillness and spoke no word without reason. When he did speak, his voice was like the warm breeze that came off the ocean with the late sunlight. Thaddeus knew that union of the mind and spirit brought things into being. He was the warmest of them all.

Judas was a powerful man with an eye for anything that was truly fine. When he was happy, he was generous, and he loved music and the things that made song. When he found a musical instrument made by inspired hands, he knew it, and he would treasure it and keep it safe. He was tireless at work and careful that all things were done as they should have been. Of the twelve, he was the only one who was not a Galilean, being a Judean.

Simon was a man of force and fire and had a mind that knew what was true and what was false no matter how subtle the covering. He was a warrior, but his knowledge of God had made him sweet and gentle. He was tall and fair, and no eye that fell upon him could resist him.

Thomas was small and slender. He was careful and thorough and had mastered the art of making things, especially from leather or coarse linen. He learned carefully and thoroughly until he knew about a thing, and then he was its master. Thomas enjoyed the conversation at the day's end and could find the error in any argument if it was there. Women loved Thomas, for they knew he would be the best of husbands, but he did not marry until my life was over.

James was called the Lesser for his small size, though the name applied in no other way. James was the happiest of the twelve, and the gleam from his light eyes was rarely missing. He had fear of nothing and enjoyed the challenge of a riddle as did no man. James seemed to dance or skip when he walked, and whenever I spoke with him, I could not help but smile. With the smile rose the bubble of joy that was his gift to impart to others. He also loved music and could play beautifully, although we could not enjoy his playing often, because our lives were preoccupied with the work at hand.

When I had chosen the twelve, we went to the foot of the mountain where I had spent the night in prayer, and a large crowd followed us, many of them from a great distance. When the twelve had settled around me and all the people had settled around them, I closed my eyes to draw the Spirit to its full attention. I instructed them, and the people around them listened. I spoke both to incite them not to be discouraged by the things of the earth that appeared to be true but were not and to teach them lasting principles: God loved the poor and the weak and would reward them. What I said was later to be called the Sermon on the Mount.

With the help of the twelve, I was well organized to deal with the large crowds of people who came to us in Capernaum, for the twelve also instructed the other disciples to teach and make the Word firm and productive in any man who sought to learn. I was proud, for around me was the beginning of the great congregation of salvation.

Some weeks later, the disciples and I were traveling to the towns around Capernaum, when we came to a town called Nain. As we entered the town, we encountered a funeral procession, and I learned that the young man who had died was the only son of a woman who had recently lost her husband as well. She was in the agony of despair; not only had she lost those she loved most, but with the loss of her son, she would face a future of uncertainty and poverty. I was moved by her grief, for she was a good woman, and the losses she'd suffered were brought upon her only by the random acts of the unkind earth. I approached her, and as she looked up at me, I saw a spark of hope reignite within her, and I told her to stop weeping.

As I approached the boy, I felt the strength of Spirit grow within me and the joy rose within my own heart at what I knew was to occur. I said to the boy,

"Young man I say to you, get up." [45] He sat up, and his body was fully restored to a clear state. He began to speak as one who woke up but did not know where he was.

Word of that miracle spread quickly throughout the whole land because raising the dead was something beyond anything they had heard of me, and it was worthy to the people of great chatter. News of the deed reached John the Baptist, who was still confined to prison, and he sent two of his disciples to me to inquire, "Are you the one who was to come, or should we expect someone else?" [46] When I heard that, I asked that my disciples spread out and bring me all the sick and infirm people they could find within the area, and when they were brought to me, I healed them all, the blind, the deaf, and the infirm. I then told John's disciples to return to him and report what they had seen.

All the good of mankind were waiting for deliverance, and John, who was the best of men, was also in hope that I, as the Son of God, which he knew I was, would exert a spiritual power dispensing instant and permanent invulnerability to those on the earth who were pushing toward and worthy of that deliverance.

I was in great pain and was wrestling with myself. Why must I be a disappointment to John and all the suffering men and women? I retired to a place of solitude and forced myself to review what was really going on. I once again tried to lay out in my mind the purpose of my life and what the future was going to be.

I knew God was the God of true justice, and that must always be true, for it was not possible for God to ever be unjust. The justice of the universe had been served upon the earth as it must be, perfectly, and that perfection showed that the conscious choice of Adam to disobey God's clear and reasonable rule—that he could have dominion over the earth and all things within it but could not eat that specific fruit—was an error. Error is not part of perfection. The condition of the earth was exactly—nothing more and nothing less than—the consequence of that action. That did not mean God and every spiritual creature in the universe were not devastated by the pain and suffering and the meaninglessness of the reality resulting from that error. They were. I was.

God warned man that if he ate of that tree, he would die, but Satan said, "You will not surely die." [47] When man ate of the tree, he brought a halt to the spiritual connection God had shared with him and an end to the arrangement God had created for man to have eternal life. Death, the instrument of renewal at work throughout the great churnings of the physical universe, was free to include man as part of its domain.

Satan stated that the rule did not serve the best interest of the creation and that God knew it: "For God knows that when you eat of it your eyes will be opened, and you will be like God, knowing good and evil." [48] Satan made it appear God did not want man to acquire this knowledge, when in truth, the entire purpose of the earth was to nurture man to spiritual immortality, which would have to include, at the proper time, knowledge of good and bad.

The first part was shown true: Adam and Eve died, as all things in error die. But would eating from the tree make man like God? Many still insisted that was true; men could be gods and goddesses. The best way to determine if God's motive in making the rule was truly for man's benefit was to see how things turned out after it was broken. If men ultimately would become gods, there might have been some argument that the rule was not in man's best interest, for despite all the pain it took to get there, man could have said, "Look. We are gods." Satan still works to convince people that they are or will be gods and goddesses.

God had allowed the choices of man and Satan to be left alone to work out their own destiny. But the truth was, that destiny would be utter ruin and suffering for the planet and for man. It had little to do with God. People on the earth were fools to think that death and suffering were part of some secret design of God.

Ultimate ruin for the planet and death and suffering for man were not conclusions satisfactory to God. However, God could not intervene without breaking his own law of perfect justice, and more importantly, though God could forgive if he wished, if he did, if he intervened, Satan could and would say that God simply did not give him enough time to work out his plans and that if God had stayed out of it, he would have brought the world to a place that was actually superior to what it was in the beginning and would have made man into godhead. Thus, nothing would be settled.

I knew there was no physical deliverance for the earth until God knew the entire universe could plainly see that regardless of what Satan said, both man and the planet were doomed. The planet was not designed to support life with man unconnected to God. When it was evident that life on the planet was beyond saving, God would be vindicated, and the words of Satan would be shown to have been lies. If man had not broken the rule, he would have been nurtured to a perfect future well precedented in the worlds of God that have existed for time upon time. Once the rule had been shown to be valid and of good intention and the premise that God may make a rule for its creation had been proven as reasonable and just, then in no other creation, physical or spiritual, throughout eternity would God have to allow such allegations as were made by Satan (or any being) concerning the earth (or anywhere) to stand. He would have been entitled to simply step in and say, "No, so-and-so creature, I have made this one rule for your benefit, and you must obey it because my integrity cannot be challenged in making this rule. Look at the record concerning earth. Satisfying your will in this case does not justify all the suffering that will come about because of your mistake." God could proceed to forgive the creature's mistake if it broke the rule anyway, or not, as he saw fit. We need never go through such a nightmare as the earth again.

So where did that leave the earth and mankind? Exactly where we were. However, as His nature was love, that was not acceptable to God, so He arranged to, without interfering with the so-called evolution of the world, still save it. That was where I came in. I came to the earth and was perfect. I had no error built in from the genetic link to Adam, and I broke no spiritual law. Yet I was to be brought to death. That would be an action of Satan's world that was equal to the mistake made by Adam, since it is God's law that no perfect thing is subject to destruction. Thus, God, through the same perfect justice that condemned Adam (and man), would be able to resurrect me from the dead. As a resurrected man, I would be a part of the world then and for all time, and the moment when the entire universe shouted, "No more! The pain of the earth is too great!" or, more mercifully, when God, in his wisdom, commanded it, I would come to that world and save it, for I was a man as well as a spirit, and I would have the right and the power to do so. I would stop its slide into nothingness, and I would rebuild it with the help of God and his faithful, atom upon atom, until every justice had been done and every wrong made right. I would reestablish man's connection to heaven, and we would joyfully resume our glorious destiny.

In that moment, I knew why I must be put to death. There was nothing new in these thoughts, but holding them all together gave me a flash of insight about my life. God would have every right to give me life again, and

I would be able to give it to mankind. I could reestablish the connection between heaven and mankind that had protected them from death at their pure beginning. When I had that realization, I remained still for a long time.

Light, love, and joy poured through me. This was the sacred secret. God was going to trick Satan. God knew Satan would hate me. God knew Satan would oppose me blindly, not knowing that my death would give God the victory and give mankind the victory. My death and lawful resurrection were all that really mattered, for there I would be, an all-powerful man who had come to that position in accord with God's own immutable laws and who was capable of exerting the full force of creation into restoring man's original destiny. All that remained was to finish my life without mistake. I wanted to get back to it.

Chapter Eight

While we were still in Nain, I received an invitation to an evening meal from a certain Pharisee named Simon. I was pleased to go, for the occasion would afford me the opportunity to discuss the things of God with not only Simon but also the many others who would attend the banquet, for he had a large and luxurious home. When I arrived, I saw that my assumption had been correct. The main room was filled with men and women, many of them Pharisees, and my position at the table had been arranged so that many of the men reclining at the tables would have the opportunity to hear what I said and to speak to me.

As I entered, however, the tone of the evening was set by the fact that I was not able to wash my feet, which was our custom. The roads were hot and dusty, and I had traveled some distance to his house. The practice was even more appropriate at such an elaborate dinner, where the furnishings and woven materials were fastidiously clean and obviously valuable and where the host had servants, as was the case there. But I was not concerned with that and took my place, enjoying the pleasant surroundings and looking forward to perhaps breaking down some of the hostility the men felt for me.

During the course of the meal, a woman approached my divan and knelt down at my feet. I looked at her as she touched my feet, and I saw that she had sinned often in the manner of having relations with men who were not her husband and had shown no remorse for her actions. As I looked at her, she began to cry, and I had pity for her, for I could see that she was a good woman and had a sorrow about her, despite her boldness. She was afraid she was ruining her life, but she did not know how to change things. As I thought those things, she began to cry with greater intensity, and her tears fell on my feet. Taking her long hair in her hands, she cried for some time and wiped the tears from my feet with her hair, drying them. Afterward, she took oil from an alabaster jar and proceeded to rub the oil onto my feet. To the people of my day, the rubbing of oil on the feet of others was a common expression of courtesy or affection, so the incident did not shock anyone in the room, but I saw from my host's eyes that he was thinking if I were a true prophet, I would know what kind of woman was touching me and reprimand her as a sinner. So I said to him, "Simon, I have something to say to you." [49]

"Teacher, say it!" He responded.

"Two men owed money to a certain moneylender," I said. "One owed him five hundred denarii, and the other fifty. Neither of them had the money to pay him back, so he canceled the debts of both. Now which of them will love him more?"

"I suppose," said Simon with an air of indifference at the seeming irrelevance of the question, "it is the one to whom he freely forgave the more."

"You judged correctly," [50] I said. Then, turning to the woman, I said to Simon, "Do you see this woman? I came into your house. You did not give me any water for my feet, but she wet my feet with her tears and wiped them with her hair. You did not give me a kiss, but this woman, from the time I entered, has not stopped kissing my feet. You did not put oil on my head, but she has poured perfume on my feet. Therefore, I tell you, her many sins have been forgiven, for she loved much. But he who has been forgiven little, loves little." [51] I again turned to the woman and said, "Your sins are forgiven." [52] The men at the table began to mumble. Who was I to forgive sins? But I said to her again, "Your faith has saved you; go your way in peace." [53] After that, the meal proceeded, but I accomplished little to further their understanding.

As I was returning to the place where we were staying, I saw the woman waiting for me, and I sent my disciple John, who had accompanied me, to bring her to me. As she approached, she was again in tears, so I asked her name, to which she answered, "Mary." I further inquired where she was from, and she told me she was from Bethany, near Jerusalem, and had a brother and sister there, Lazarus and Martha. She had left the place because they had grown angry with her because of her sinning. I told her to return to her home and tell them all that had happened; they would accept her.

After those events, I went throughout Galilee as if in a great circuit. I took with me my twelve, and others traveled with us to help and to learn. Many of them were people I had cured, and they were grateful and had faith in what I was doing and in who I was. There were also women who went along with us, and they provided for us with their own possessions and were a source of strength to us. We traveled from village to village, and I cured many. The controversy about us became great, and many scribes and Pharisees came to us from Jerusalem, though, in the most part, simply to discredit us. Even my brothers came out to find me. They had heard about all the things that were going on, and they wanted to lay hold of me and force me to return to Nazareth because they were of the opinion that I had lost my mind. However, because I was healing those with incurable diseases, it was difficult for even the Pharisees to deny the power of the Spirit. They began to say I was casting out demons in the name of Beelzebub, a common name for Satan. Despite my pointing out the impossibility of that being the case, they persisted in saying such things, and I observed that Spirit itself had a great anger for those men because of the things they were saying. Although I could come to forgive them, they had become condemned, for Spirit would not forgive them, because they spoke against the Spirit.

I continued teaching, and the people received me well because they were being cured and because their lives were tiresome, and my words gave them hope. But I was concerned, for I knew that when I was gone, it would be difficult for them to remember with faith, for they were not getting the meaning of my words. So I began to teach them with illustrations, hoping that by my speaking in that fashion, they might remember my words and continue to think about the things I told them, as a man might do with a riddle. I first gave them the illustration of the seed that was cast, pointing out how some of it would grow, and some of it would not. That illustration was based specifically on the results I had seen with the many we had taught; although they heard the Word, for one reason or another, many would not produce the fruit of the teaching. I knew that at the center of their resistance was the fact that without the religion of the land embracing my words, the heart of the people had absorbed almost all that it could sustain. We did not give up, however, but continued to teach with increased resolve, for if even one heard, understood, and came to know and believe the truth, the reward was worth the effort.

I had been teaching for some two years, and I wanted to reach as many as I could before the obstacles I saw in my path prevented me from giving further knowledge to the people. I divided the twelve into twos and sent them out to wherever they could go within Israel to talk in the synagogues, on the roadways, and at the doors of the households of the land. I sent Spirit with them and told them not to prepare with either gold or sword, for the things they needed would be provided. If they preached in an area and were not well received, I instructed them to continue on, leaving nothing of their hope behind and not looking back. However, in many areas, they were well received, for people were curious because of all the wonderful things they had heard, and I had given the disciples the power to drive out demons and cure the sick. Their faith was strong and they were able to speak strong words, full of power, and heal.

Just before our third Passover together, I was awaiting the return of my disciples so we could prepare for our journey to Jerusalem, when I heard that John the Baptist had been beheaded. I was deeply grieved when his disciples brought me the news, and for three days, I retired to solitude—not to set a model for any behavior but because I wished to be alone with my God and my sorrow.

Soon the twelve returned to Capernaum, and they were full of enthusiasm when they saw me, for they all had stories to tell and wanted me to know all the wonderful things they had accomplished. Well, as soon as they arrived at the house, the crowds began to gather, and although the disciples were tired and hungry, I knew we would not be able to have a meal together in peace. I told them to prepare the boat, and we headed off for a place where we could be alone and they could have the pleasure of comparing their journeys and experiences, as they deserved.

When we landed, a crowd had already gathered, for some had seen us leave and had run along the shore, and others had followed. As we made our way up the hillside, the crowd grew, and soon there were more than five thousand men and as many women and children. It was mid-afternoon, and the disciples quickly grew concerned that the people would soon be getting hungry, as most of them had come a long way. I told them to give the people something to eat, and I asked Philip where we should buy bread. Philip laughed and exclaimed with a great, good-humored snort, "Why, it would require two hundred days' wages for just a little for each!"

Andrew, who could always find the beginning of a thread, said, "This small boy has five loaves and two fishes, but what are these among so many?" It was springtime, so I had the disciples tell the multitude to seat themselves on the lush green grass over the land. They sat down in groups of fifty and a hundred. I took the loaves with the two fish, and I looked up to the heavens and asked my Father to bless the food. Then I began breaking it up and giving pieces to the disciples so they could put the food in baskets and distribute it to the people. I felt the love of the Spirit moving through me and noticed that after I had distributed a portion, as my hand returned to the linen the food was wrapped in, the original amount remained inside.

After the crowd had eaten, they began to talk, for they knew what had happened, and they planned together to lift me up and make me king. I saw what they had in mind, and although their intentions were good, those people had no authority to make me king, and such an act would only have led to disaster when word reached Jerusalem and Rome. I dismissed the crowd and ordered the disciples to go to the boat and cast off for Capernaum. Knowing the people would not accept my dismissal, I cloaked myself and went to the top of the mountain.

Just before dawn, I looked out over the sea. The moon was bright as it waxed toward the full moon of the upcoming Passover. The wind was strong over the water, and I saw the boat heading against the waves. All twelve were rowing with difficulty, and they were making no progress. It was about three miles to their position, and I walked down the mountain and out over the sea toward them. I continued walking past the boat, and when they saw me, they exclaimed in fright, thinking I was an apparition. I called out to them to have no fear, as it was indeed me they saw. Peter quickly stood up and said. "Lord, if it is you, command me to come to you over the waters."

"Come," [54] I said. Peter immediately came out of the boat and began walking over the water toward me, but feeling the windstorm, he became afraid and began to sink. I was proud of Peter but was in no way inclined to give him praise for giving up certainty in an act of faith before it was complete, so I corrected him for his giving way to doubt and pulled him from the water. Together we walked to the boat and boarded it.

After we were aboard, the wind subsided, and I mildly instructed the men to continue on our way, for they were frozen by the events, not knowing whether to be afraid or exuberant. My words broke the spell, and after glancing quickly at each other with nervous grins and whispered comments about my being indeed the Son of God, they quickly returned to the task of rowing, as there was no wind. We soon came to Gennesaret, where James and John's parents lived.

After anchoring the boat, we made our way to the shore, where we relaxed and ate from the leftovers of the previous evening. The disciples were numb, in a kind of euphoria. They had come face-to- face with such tangible proof of the power of things spiritual that even though their minds had already believed in the truth of such things, they were overloaded with faith, not knowing if they were in a dream and would soon wake up or what would happen next. It was only a short time before we were seen, and many people came to us, bringing their sick. I cured them, and the men fell into a routine more familiar to them, with the events of the last few hours slipping into the manageable confines of memory.

When we reached Capernaum, much of the crowd who had been with us the night before came to us, and they were indignant that we had left them, asking us when we had arrived back. I admonished them, for I knew they merely wanted us to feed them again, so they asked me, "What must we do to do the works God requires?"

"The work of God is this," I said. "To believe in the one he has sent." [55] But the crowd was not satisfied, and they asked what sign I would perform so they could see it and believe in me.

At that point, the two main streams of activity in my life since my baptism began to merge. I had been teaching the people, and I had been trying to reason with the priests. I saw that in terms of teaching the great crowds of people, I could go no further, because to do so, I would have to assume the role of God's appointed leader in the tradition of Moses, allowing them to lift me up as their king and accepting the role. To do so without the blessing of the priests would have been an act of presumption on my part, an act against God himself, for the rulers of the nation had been ordained by his law. As a descendant of David, I had a right to be made the king of Israel, but to become such, I would need to be sanctified by the anointed priests of God through their recognition of the will of God and their acting in his name.

That did not mean I would stop teaching the people of the land, if for no other reason than my disciples needed to gain experience in teaching so that when I was gone, they would be able to continue the work with or without the priesthood. But I saw clearly that my ability to keep the good faith of the average man would now begin to diminish unless I made progress with the men of power.

Seeing those underlying forces at work, I was not surprised when the crowd pointed out, disputing my admonition that all they wanted was food, that Moses had given the people heavenly bread, the manna in the wilderness. Since I was now aware that our interchange had taken on a new dimension, with the convergence of the parallel avenues of teaching now limiting my ability to influence the people, I was prepared to answer them directly, as I would the Pharisees, and I pointed out that manna was not truly a heavenly thing, as it was fabricated from the natural things of the earth, and that God, not Moses, had given it to them. Since the question was to the point, I continued by saying that God indeed had given them the bread from heaven: the One who had come down to them from heaven to give life to the world. "Lord, always give us that bread," [56] the people responded.

There was no reason to turn back, and I said point-blank that I was the bread. I said that he who came to me would not get hungry, and the one who believed in me would not get thirsty. But they had seen me and still did not believe, I told them. I explained that the Father had given me the world, and thus, that world would one day become mine, along with the ability to give life; also, I would not reject anyone who came to me. I had come to earth to do the will of God, and his will was that I lose nothing out of the world but resurrect it all at the last day, for the will of God was that everyone who understood me and exercised faith in me should have everlasting life.

After I said those things, the crowd grew agitated, saying things like "Is this not Jesus, the son of Joseph?" [57] But I told them to stop murmuring, and I continued to say that no man could believe in me unless God allowed it through Spirit, and the ones who did believe me I would resurrect at the beginning of the new world. I pointed out that the prophets had promised, "They will all be taught by God," and I continued to explain that everyone who had looked for God and learned from God would come to me. I further told them that no one had seen God except the One who came from God and that I was telling the truth when I said that he who believed would get everlasting life by believing.

I did not stop. I reminded them that their forefathers ate manna in the wilderness, but they died. "But here is bread that comes from heaven so that if a man eats this bread, he will not die." I ended by saying, "I am the living bread that came down from heaven. If anyone eats of this bread, he will live forever. This bread is my flesh, which I will give for the life of the world." [58] That was enough, and the crowd dispersed, thinking and muttering their discontent.

The next day was the Sabbath, and I went to the synagogue to take part in the service and talk, as was now my custom when I was in Capernaum. I knew that regardless of what I said, my progress with the people at large had reached its apex. The true conflict was now taking place in the spiritual world between Satan, who acted through the men who ruled in God's name but lay under the power of darkness, and the Spirit of God as it manifested through me and, to a lesser degree, my followers. I did not hold back but spoke to the matter that was in everyone's heart. I began by saying, "I tell you the truth, unless you eat the flesh of the Son of Man and drink his blood, you have no life in you." [59]

It was abundantly evident from the nature of our religion, the nature of all of my actions on the earth, and the symbolic and sacred nature of bread and blood throughout our scriptures, not to mention simple common sense, that what I had said was simply a metaphor. However, the perversity of the reaction to my words was as understandable as the reaction of the Pharisees to my healing on the Sabbath or the elders of Nazareth attempting to take my life, so I was not concerned that the metaphor I used was open to base interpretations, because the people would understand or not based on the condition of their hearts, and despite their directness, the words were the absolute truth. The reaction of the crowd was bad, to say the least. Was I a priest of darkness to talk of drinking blood and eating human flesh? Even some of my disciples made no effort to understand but concurred with the general feelings of the crowd that this sort of speech was shocking, saying, "This is a hard teaching. Who can accept it?" [60]

Satan had found an opening to exploit the human propensity to doubt. The fears and insecurities of the people were excited to the point where rationality gave way to negativity. Faith and understanding sometimes require effort, and there was little inclination for that here, where outrage and judgment were flowing without thought or restraint. It can be a relief to abandon thoughts that go against the grain of existing public opinion, and here was an opportunity to do that. Many of my disciples left and did not continue to follow me.

I turned to the twelve and said, "You do not want to leave too, do you?" [61] Peter replied, "Lord, to whom shall we go? You have the words of eternal life. We believe and know that you are the Holy One of God." [62] The twelve remained, but I saw that Judas had stumbled.

For all men, the truth can be a difficult thing, and Satan will try every man. Those on earth today who think my teachings will bring about only kindness and compassion in their lives should remember the following of my sayings: "No servant is greater than his master. If they persecuted me, they will persecute you also. If they obeyed my teaching, they will obey yours also. They will treat you this way because of my name, for they do not know the One who sent me" [63] and "Do you think I came to bring peace on earth? No, I tell you, but division. From now on there will be five in one family divided against each other, three against two and two against three. They will be divided, father against son and son against father, mother against daughter and daughter against mother, mother-in-law against daughter-in-law and daughter-in-law against mother-in-law." [64]

The cycles of the earth are deep. Each turn of the spire is different from the one before but similar to that which is above and below in its pattern. These patterns pick up all that occurs as they progress and manifest the results in the corresponding segment of the next cycle. The influences on each segment, or moment, are constantly changing according to other factors and forces. It appears we get the sense of being able to almost anticipate what is to come next, but there are so many subtle variations it is beyond the mind's ability to contain it all.

This moment in my teaching was unexpected. My nature was love, and I had proceeded using my nature as my direction, but the sum of my actions was now being displayed in a cycle of hard reality. Despite the truth of my words, the truth of my healing, and the importance of my message, at that moment, the result was cold and thin. The earth, in its imperfect human understanding, had absorbed me and was unimpressed and perhaps even unchanged, except for a few.

Chapter Nine

Within the week, we left for Jerusalem and the Passover to continue with what was now the work: engaging the Pharisees. The trip was fruitless, however, for I had to be cautious, as my life was in danger everywhere. Nonetheless, we spent the festival in the Holy City, and it was important to me that my disciples and I be there together on that night. I would not give up trying to turn the minds of the Pharisees, and it was not my time to die. After the days were over, we returned to Galilee and continued our efforts to teach and heal.

Many scribes and Pharisees from Jerusalem followed us to Capernaum, looking for grounds on which to accuse me of breaking the law. They would twist the law to try to make my actions or words appear to be a violation of the law of Moses. But what grounds they found only sprang from their own traditions, and Spirit deflected the accusations. The rules and traditions that had been written down over the last handful of generations had begun to make a mockery of the law, which, more than anything else, they now used as an instrument of power for their own benefit. The law no longer had much to do with God, for they worshipped God with their lips, but their hearts were far from him. What they held up to be the doctrine of the truth was in fact little more than the commands of men, used to exert and hold power over other men. Perhaps many of the leaders had made the progress to this state of corruption with the best of intentions, supposedly for the good of the people. The intoxication that occurs when men experience the power that comes from exerting what is, in the beginning, genuine spiritual authority is apparently irresistible to most. It is Satan's most effective weapon in his battle against the truth, and there is not a religion on the face of the earth that has not fallen prey to such corruption. The reason this corruption is so insidious is that it appears in the form of righteousness.

When a man becomes acquainted with the fact that God exists and, in fact, lives in the same moment as he himself, he wants to exert all his strength to come closer to God and to please God. He does good works and is acknowledged by his fellow man. He disciplines himself and becomes strong in his habits. These men come naturally to leadership. The problem is that the dilemma of the earth is more complex than simply mastering a few of the most obvious obstacles that face us all. One of the complexities that ensures our continued enslavement to being and doing wrong is that time is a real and unrelenting part of our lives.

The path seems clear for a man who begins to understand God and finds some happiness in extricating himself from the most obvious snares that face us all. However, as time passes, the man becomes concerned that others have not mastered their own natures as well as he has. As time grinds away, these concerns grow. These other men appear to be in the way of his happiness; in the way of the happiness of the earth; and, most to the point, in God's way. This creates a natural conflict, and the trap is that the easy answer to this conflict seems to be found in the need to change the behavior of the other men. After all, this appears to be what God wants. Since these disciplined men are often leaders, they find allies in men like themselves, and together they find success in controlling others, which they mistakenly think is the will of God. It's such a simple thing. It is not a credit to mankind that the dark forces have been able to use this simple half truth to manipulate men with such ease that any real movement toward God on the part of an expanding group of sincere men can easily be transformed into a debacle. The well-intentioned leaders are quickly transformed from seekers and sowers of truth to sowers of division and hatred. In the defense of such men, it can be said that their strong desire for a simple and straightforward path to deliverance is a worthy master, but that is merely another half truth and does nothing to save the man using such logic from the fact that he has fallen from the path.

God gives the gifts of purity and discipline to all men who seek them with sincerity, effort, and prayer, but such a gift is its own reward. When the goodness of a man leads to his resentment of others, it is time for him to return to the beginning, to humility and solitude. Being strong in the knowledge of God's law is never an excuse for allowing oneself to indulge in the sin of judging another man in the name of God. But such is the nature and strength of the dark spirit that rules the earth that man is easily turned against his fellow man, and no iniquity or act of violence or unthinkable cruelty is too great to be perpetuated in the name of God.

This is what I faced.

The disciples were exhausted by the unreasoning and unrelenting opposition of the leaders of our religion, and so was I. After some discussion, we planned a trip that would afford us time to relax, build up strength, and enjoy ourselves. We headed for the regions of Tyre and Sidon, some miles to the north. I instructed the men to keep our whereabouts secret. In all the time we taught, that was the only trip we made outside the land of Israel. We paid for the use of a house near Sidon, and after a refreshing stay, we headed south again, on foot, and then east across the headwaters of the Jordan to the region of Decapolis. Although that was primarily a gentile area, many hundreds and then thousands of Jews came to hear us and be taught. Once again, the crowds became large, and when they were running out of food, for many had been with us in the countryside for two or three days, I felt sorry for them and fed them. However, such miraculous food was not the object of the message I had to give, so we traveled once again to the Sea of Galilee, where we boarded a boat and crossed over to the western shore, hoping to return to Capernaum. Immediately, we encountered a large group of Pharisees and Sadducees from Jerusalem, who demanded I perform a great sign for them as a signal of my authenticity. There was neither goodness of intention nor room for truth in their minds, so I warned them that they were a wicked generation and that the only sign they would see was the sign of Jonah, which I used to represent the three days I would spend in the bowels of the earth before I was resurrected, just as Jonah had spent three days in the stomach of the fish before he was disgorged.

We returned to the boat and headed for the northeast tip of the sea, to a place known as Bethsaida. From there, we headed north, at the direction of Spirit, toward the district of Caesarea Philippi. There the land sloped continually upward until it came to an area high above the rest of the countryside. It was only about thirty miles from the water, but the continual ascent made for slow walking, and the climb took us two days. I was now certain my death was not far off, so I was pensive, wanting to make sure I had left nothing unsaid or undone between the twelve and myself. On the way, I instructed Peter about things to come, and I entrusted him to begin the new congregation I would establish on the earth, for I also knew with some assurance that Israel was to be cut off, and teaching would have to go on without the great organization of the Living God, the religion of the priests of Judah.

I knew it was time to tell the disciples in plain words that I was going to face suffering and death at the hands of the Jews. They did not accept it well, for they knew I had power to avoid death at the hands of men, and they could not understand why I would choose to allow such a thing to happen. Everything we had done on our great adventure pointed to a happy ending by the reckonings of men and their fables, and although that was to be ultimately true, they never really understood why it had to be the way it was, until I brought them understanding from the other side of death. A number of my close followers had joined us on the trek to the mountain, and I had time to warn them as we walked that to follow me was a difficult path. I told them they should be prepared to leave everything behind, even life itself, if they chose to continue following me.

I could see the distress of my disciples as they struggled to understand why I must be put to death, especially Peter and John, who I think in some way felt they must have let me down and perhaps could have done, or could do, something to alter my unhappy fate. I could have tried harder, I suppose, to explain the necessity of what was to happen, but I did not. The truth was that the full understanding of the sacred secret was not to become fully clear— even, in a sense, to me—until after I was resurrected.

My death had the potential to free the ultimate destiny of mankind from the grip of death and slavery forever. But as we walked toward the mountain, that had not yet occurred. I still had to reach the point of death and be worthy of resurrection by God, which meant that should I make a mistake, any mistake at all, between any moment along my path and the final second of my life, I would have accomplished nothing except a lot of magical things and a lot of talk, none of which would have helped mankind one iota in the long run. We would have had to start over with some other plan to save the earth.

As the Son of God, I was going to succeed, but Satan is powerful on the earth, and had he known exactly what was going on, he might have acted differently, to the increased suffering and despair of the world. The sacred secret was to remain just that—a secret—until all things were complete. Thus, Spirit veiled the complete understanding of it from every living creature except God until its completion. It was not a play that the disciples and I simply walked through; it was the living moment of the true universal reality, and as such, on the earth, the next moment was primarily based on the choices and actions of the one before. Just as God did not will the fall of the earth, he could not simply will the deliverance of the earth. It had to be earned as it had been lost: by action. Any slip on my part could mean all was lost.

I did know then, with the full power of my being, what I should do at every moment, and a few moments later, I separated John, Peter, and James from the others and proceeded to walk with them toward the top of Mount Hermon.

It was almost dusk when we began making our way up the side of the mountain. Spirit allowed me to make sure the weather was perfect, although I did not have to do so consciously. As we climbed, our thoughts became linked to our ascent, and the journey grew more and more spiritual as we went. Our concentration filtered out the noise of baser thoughts and shook off any collected bits of doubt or confusion. A stumble and a quick look down reminded us to clear our minds of any lack of faith and allow Spirit to guide our climb. It was about midnight when we reached as high as we were going to go, and the three found places to sit, catch their breath, and gaze around at the beauty of the heights. I went a few paces away to my own spot, and after looking about, I began to pray.

I had been in prayer for a while, when I felt Spirit increase its intensity within me. I opened my eyes to see that my body was shining with a bright white light. I stood up, and as I did, the disciples sat up, for they had been falling asleep. My entire body was now replaced by light, although my form stayed intact, and I was intensely alive, as if I were in the higher worlds. As I turned my head, I saw two equally bright figures, and I recognized them to be angels, although they appeared in the form of Moses and Elijah. I knew they were not the actual prophets, but they explained to me that for the sake of my followers, they would appear as symbols they knew. The angels talked to me about my departure, by which they meant my upcoming death, which also was for the benefit of the three—so they might see and know that my death would be neither an end nor something to be avoided but a time of great spiritual fulfillment.

As the angels moved away, Peter hurried over to ask if he could prepare a tent for each of us. I almost laughed, and if my smile could have been brighter than the light of which I was composed, it would have been. At that moment, a luminous fog surrounded us, and we heard the voice of God: "This is my Son, whom I love; with him I am well pleased. Listen to him!" [65] I looked again to the three, and they were on the ground in fear, so I went to them, raised them up, and told them to be not afraid but at peace. We spent the rest of the night on the mountain. The fog had disappeared with the angels, so we slept under the bright sky. The stars seemed immediate and living, as if to remind us of the nature of the light I had been composed of only a few minutes before. The disciples rested, again in a kind of euphoria. I was at peace as well, for I knew that Spirit had provided a rare and transcendent moment that would not only benefit the teaching to come and the fulfillment of scripture but also give my friends a living memory that would ease their pain in a way that the best of words could not.

In the morning, we walked down to the camp of my followers, which was near a small town at the base of the mountain. As we approached the town, we could see that something was wrong. My disciples were there, arguing with a group of scribes, and as I approached, I asked them what the dispute was about. The townsfolk had brought a boy to my disciples to be cured. The boy had been possessed of a demon since childhood, and although they'd tried, my disciples had not been able to dispel it. The scribes were delighting in their failure and were busy criticizing the friends. "Oh unbelieving generation," I said, "how long shall I stay with you? How long shall I put up with you?" [66] I said this for the benefit of the scribes. I asked the boy's father to bring him to me, but as the youth approached, the demon who possessed him threw him to the ground in a great convulsion. I questioned the father, who appealed to me with great urgency and great faith. I threw out the demon and revived the boy, who was exhausted to the point of death. When the boy's father had been begging me for help, he had asked me if I could indeed help. I had responded that all things could be for one who had faith, to which he said, "I do believe; help me overcome my unbelief!" [67] That was a wise thing for him to say, and in a way, it answered the question of why the disciples had not been able to cure the boy. Later, when they asked me why they were unable to do so despite having done such things before, I explained to them that it was a powerful spirit, and they should have resorted to prayer to strengthen their own faith. Once again, I stressed that faith was the key to all works and added that increasing faith was a work of its own.

I wished to return home to Capernaum, and on the way, I made certain we went unnoticed by traveling through towns and villages during the night and requesting that Spirit keep our identities veiled. I wanted to make it clear to the men what was going to happen in the near future, for although I was sure of those things, they were still resisting knowing. I said directly, "The Son of Man is going to be betrayed into the hands of men. They will kill him, and on the third day he will be raised to life." [68] Even after that, they were unclear on the matter, but they were afraid to question me about it further, so I said no more, and we continued on our way to Capernaum.

The wind of Spirit had shifted, and the land lay quiet, as if watching to see what might become of me. My disciples and I had time to sit, meditate, and reflect on things in a traditional way. We discussed many things, including the things of human nature and the little things we had put aside in the intense and relentless work we had been doing. The disciples squabbled about who among them was the greatest, and I corrected them for missing the point that in all likelihood, the least of men on the earth had the best chance of being correct in the true reality. I also reminded them of what they knew full well from meditation: one had to be innocent and receptive to have union with Spirit. It was important for us to talk about that kind of thing, for when I was gone, so would be the great spiritual center that kept those around me from slipping back to the limits set by the mundane trials all men go through on a daily basis. I gave them guidelines concerning how to deal with their fellow men, knowing they would pass such advice on to those they were to teach in the coming years.

It was a peaceful time, perhaps a small gift from my Father. Even my brothers came to visit me from Nazareth. Although they still did not understand that I was the Son of Man, as they all would eventually, they nonetheless wanted me to succeed in what they perceived as my attempt to become famous. With that in mind, they urged me to go to Jerusalem for the upcoming Festival of Tabernacles, thinking our temporarily quiet time was a waste of time and pointing out, "No one who wants to become a public figure acts in secret." [69] They were not aware of the gravity of the situation, and I insisted my disciples make nothing known to them or my mother about what was to occur. But I did respond to them that the world hated me because I made it known that its works were wicked, and I told them to go ahead with the traveling parties about to leave for Jerusalem. Several days later, the disciples and I left for the festival without telling anyone, taking the less traveled route through Samaria, as I had done on my trip to the temple when I was young.

It had now been three years since John had baptized me, and many things had taken place. At the festival, the crowds were wondering about me, asking, "Where is that man?" [70] and debating about who I was. Some insisted I was a good man, and others were certain I was misleading them. Yet no man spoke out publicly in my favor, even those who had been cured, for they were in fear of the anger of the priests.

The Festival of Tabernacles was the great harvest feast. It was a time of great rejoicing for the people and lasted for seven days. We arrived about halfway through the celebrations, and we immediately made our way to the temple, where I began to teach. I spoke for a long time, and the crowd received my words well. Many of the crowd were travelers from throughout all Israel and the lands around, as was the case at all festivals, and they did not know that the rulers had planned to kill me. Despite that, I talked about the Pharisees desiring my death, which confused many, but I wanted to make one all-important point, and it related to my persecution: "Stop judging by mere appearances, and make a right judgment." [71] The world, to this day, has not listened to this command.

Although the visitors to the city knew nothing of the plans against me, the people of Judea did, for the priests had not been able to keep their intentions secret, and gossip had made their objective a much-discussed matter. Many wondered if the fact that I had not been captured might mean the rulers had accepted that I was the Christ. The Pharisees were trying hard to convince the people of Judea that I could not be the Christ, and one method they used was to stress that I was a Galilean, for the Judeans had a saying: "Nothing good can come out of Galilee." The Pharisees knew I had been born in Bethlehem, but they kept that from the people to serve their own purposes. When the crowd of Judeans began to challenge me on that point, albeit without scriptural correctness, asking how a Galilean could be the Anointed One, I responded with the truth. After clarifying the prophecies that related to their questions, I added that the real problem was that they did not know God, which infuriated them, and they tried to seize me to take me to the authorities, but I escaped.

Despite the hostility generated by those who hated me, many came to have faith in me and pointed out all I had done, saying, "When the Christ comes, will he do more miraculous signs than this man?" [72] When the Pharisees heard the people saying that sort of thing, they immediately sent out soldiers to arrest me. I knew that, but I kept on speaking. There were several incidents. When the soldiers would arrive, they would listen to me, and on seeing the crowd also listening, they would not arrest me, for they themselves were not certain in their hearts that I was not the Christ. They would avoid arresting me, saying to each other that it was not a good time, and so it went.

On the seventh day of the festival, I was still preaching on the steps of the temple. I explained to the people, with great emotion and spirit, who I was and why I had come, and I offered them the water of life. Many accepted me, but others did not, and disputes arose as I spoke. The soldiers, who had come again, still could not find it in their hearts to arrest me, and they returned to the Pharisees and the chief priests. The priests were in great anger when they saw that I had not been captured, and they chastised the soldiers. They would not listen to anyone, even from among themselves, who would speak in my defense, so great was their hatred.

After the soldiers had left, I proceeded deeper into the temple, to the court of women, which was the innermost court allowing women and children, and continued to teach. On each night of the festival, four massive lampstands were placed and lit in that sanctuary. Each lampstand was supplied by four huge basins of oil, so the light was immense, illuminating not only the temple but also the whole vicinity. Even there, the Pharisees challenged me, and that continued throughout the evening and the next day. I spent most of the next day in argument, for I was earnestly trying to reason with them, to no avail. Finally, they became enraged and picked up stones to hurl at me, but I hid from them by allowing Spirit to confuse their vision, and I left the temple.

Although the festival was over, we did not leave Jerusalem but decided to stay through the next Sabbath. On the Sabbath, we were walking through the city, when Andrew noticed a boy who had been blind since birth, and he asked me who had sinned—the boy or his parents? He asked the question because many rabbis taught that a child could sin in the womb—a clumsy grappling with the truth of man's inescapable condition. I told him that neither the boy nor his parents had sinned and that the boy's infirmity was going to become involved in the working out of the will of God. To cure the boy, I used a ritual that I knew would be familiar to him and give him faith, and when he returned from the Pool of Siloam, as I had instructed, he could see. He began to rejoice and would not stop, and some of his neighbors did not believe it was him, thinking, "This is a man who looks like him." When they realized it was the same boy, they took him to their synagogue and told the Pharisees what had happened. The Pharisees asked the boy what had happened, but upon hearing his testimony, they said of me, "This man is not from God, for he does not keep the Sabbath." The neighbors asked them, "Why not?" (meaning, "Why is he not from God?"), and the Pharisees replied, "Because he does not observe the Sabbath." [73]

But some of the Pharisees wondered how a man could do such things and not be a man of God, and they were divided. They asked the boy what he thought, and the boy replied, "He is a prophet." [74] They could not believe that, and they thought there was some kind of plot between the boy and me, so they summoned the boy's parents.

The parents knew that anyone expressing faith in me would be expelled from the synagogue and that the cutting off of such fellowship amounted to exclusion from the community at large, which could spell disaster for the poor couple, so they were cautious. The Pharisees asked them if the boy was their son who had been born blind, and if so, how was it that he could now see? The parents replied that yes, he was their son who had been born blind, but they did not want to say they knew why he could now see, so they asked the Pharisees to ask the boy himself, pointing out that he was of age. The Pharisees called the boy again and tried to intimidate him, saying they had evidence I was a sinner, and they demanded the boy give glory to God. The boy replied boldly, for he had been a beggar all his life and was used to being pushed around: "Whether he is a sinner or not, I don't know. One thing I do know. I was blind but now I see!" [75] The Pharisees wanted to find a flaw in the boy's story, so they asked him again what I had done to restore his sight. The boy, being who he was, replied, "I have told you already and you did not listen. Why do you want to hear it again?" and he added for his own pleasure, "Do you want to become his disciples, too?" [76]

Of course, the Pharisees were enraged, and they hurled insults at him and said, "You are this fellow's disciple! We are disciples of Moses! We know that God spoke to Moses, but as for this fellow, we don't even know where he comes from." [77]

Now, as I said, the boy was not afraid of men, for they had done all they could to him, so he spoke his mind, which was a good one. "Now that is remarkable! You don't know where he comes from, yet he opened my eyes. We know that God does not listen to sinners. He listens to the Godly man who does his will. Nobody has ever heard of opening the eyes of a man born blind. If this man were not from God, he could do nothing."

They replied, "You were steeped in sin at birth; how dare you lecture us!" [78] Then they threw him out, expelling him from the synagogue.

When I learned what they had done to the boy, I sought him out, and I asked him, "Do you believe in the son of man?" [79]

He said, "Who is he, sir? [80] Tell me so that I may believe in him." [81]

I replied, "You have now seen him; in fact, he is the one speaking to you." [82]

The boy bowed before me and said with all sweetness, "I do put faith in him, Lord." [83]

I then said for the sake of the Pharisees who were listening, "For this judgement I came into this world: that those not seeing might see and those seeing might become blind." [84]

The Pharisees immediately said, "What? Are we blind too?" [85]

I wanted them to know the difference between the sins made simply from human weakness and the sins made with a hardened mind, so I said, "If you were blind, you would not be guilty of sin, but now that you claim that you can see, your guilt remains." [86]

Chapter Ten

When we left Jerusalem, we did not head home to Galilee but remained in the countryside around the capital. The great majority of my teaching had been in Galilee, so I determined to stay in Judea and focus our attention there and on Perea, which lay on the east side of the Jordan, for the people there had not had much chance to hear us.

I called all my disciples to me. There were about two hundred, and of those, I chose seventy. I divided the seventy into groups of two, and I sent them out ahead of us wherever we planned to go. I gave them the power to cure the sick and instructed them to do so.

When the followers returned to me, they reported all that had happened. They were filled with surprise and happiness at what they had accomplished. "Lord, even the demons submit to us in your name," [87] they would say, and I was made to know everything that had been done.

When they had all come in, I felt a great joy, for I knew that even after I left the earth, the teaching was secure and would be continued with the power of Spirit, and it would succeed. I prayed to my Father, expressing my great gratitude for what he had allowed, and I was again filled with joy and the power of the spirit. Turning to my disciples, I said, "Blessed are the eyes that see what you see. For I tell you that many prophets and kings wanted to see what you see but did not see it, and to hear what you hear but did not hear it." [88] I was, truthfully, a little surprised at the great things those simple and humble people had achieved, for the twelve had not gone with them, so I said aloud, "I praise you, Father, Lord of heaven and earth, because you have hidden these things from the wise and learned, and revealed them to little children. Yes, Father, for this was your good pleasure." [89]

The Spirit was brightly alive on the earth, but it was not from me that the great energy came; my disciples and my followers were the source of that power because I had granted it to them. I realized then that no one would get this power without my granting it, but when I did, it could be used to good effect. I was doubly happy, for I now knew the teachings could not be defeated, even by the dark one himself.

After that, a change came to my teaching, for I became drawn to Jerusalem, and I could not look away. I began to tell my disciples all the things I wanted them to know and wanted recorded in scripture, because I knew I did not have much time.

I began a slow spiral toward Jerusalem and the fulfillment of my work. I would approach the city, and I would move away, seeing the time was not right. I would withdraw only to approach again. Many Pharisees would come out to challenge me, test me, and try to catch me up, but it was not entirely of their own volition, for they had been moved to do and say those things so that I might issue the last warnings to Israel and prophesy regarding the things that were to come regarding the end of God's singular relationship with Israel and the beginning of a new chosen people to be taken from all the nations of the earth.

I made appearances in all the villages around Jerusalem and in Jericho, Bethany, and Bethphage. My disciples and I would go past Bethany to the Mount of Olives, and we would withdraw. All the time, I would issue warnings to Israel and speak metaphors concerning the things to come. I was troubled, for I was a Jew, and like all Jews, I longed for the day when Israel and God would be united in a time of joy and prosperity, and I could see that was not to be. My heart broke for the nation, and I suffered that I could not reach out to them, bring them to me, and give them the glory and the riches of the kingdom of heaven. I continued to go around and into Jerusalem, and each time, we came into danger, yet it was not the time, so we withdrew.

Finally, I went off to pray by myself, and it was given to me that we should depart. The next day, we began to travel, and we headed north and crossed over the Jordan into the area of Perea. After a time, we came to the spot where John used to baptize, and we made camp there, for I had been directed to come there. It had been almost three and a half years since I had made my way out of the pool I now gazed down upon. The memories flooded over me, and I remembered how I had been filled with the Spirit of the kingdom of the heavens as I emerged from the water and how my presence had shaken the foundations of the earth with the power of the Kingdom of God. I was quiet, and soon the memories joined with the present. I was heavy with emotion as I reviewed all that had happened since that day, but I prayed, and the sorrow and the sweetness subsided. I walked back to the camp in a kind of numbness, a kind of emptiness.

Soon the people of the surrounding towns became aware of us, and they came to us to see. They brought their sick, and we cured them. Many of them came to believe that I was the Son of God, for they knew that John had not performed a single miracle but had foretold my coming.

We also traveled to some of the out of the way places around our camp, and we were in such a place, a nearby village, when a man came stumbling into the room, exhausted from his journey. He had brought word that Lazarus, the brother of Mary, was sick. I had come to know Mary, the woman who had washed my feet with her tears, after she had returned to

Bethany, as I had instructed her. She had remained in Bethany with her sister, Martha, and her brother, Lazarus, ever since. They had all become believers and were devoted to me, so we often stayed with them when we were in the vicinity of Jerusalem. Lazarus was a good man. He was slight and had the features considered classic to my people. He was a man with a quiet self-assurance that sprang, I think, from an irresistible sense of humor. I had become fond of him, as I had his sisters. Martha was strikingly beautiful and equally strong, with untiring energy and competence that she put to the task of seeing to the needs of others. Of all the people on the earth, next to my family and the twelve, those three knew me best as a man.

We gave the messenger something to eat, and I reassured him, telling him to rest and return to Bethany. Two days went by, and then I said to the disciples, "Let us go back into Judea." [90]

They were amazed and said, "A short while ago the Jews tried to stone you, and yet you are going back there?" [91] They said that because they were content with the peace of where we were, but I explained to them that there was a time to do things and a time not to, and it was a time to do things.

Then I hinted to them about Lazarus, but they did not understand, so I said clearly, "Lazarus is dead." [92] They became dejected, but Thomas soon stood and began to prepare for the trip, saying with a note of resigned humor, "Let us also go, that we may die with him," [93] referring to the danger that awaited me if I returned to Jerusalem.

We arrived at Bethany without incident. Lazarus had been in the tomb for four days, having died even as the messenger was returning. As we approached the house, Martha came out to meet me and said, "Lord, if you had been here my brother would not have died. But I know that even now God will give you whatever you ask."

I said to her, "Your brother will rise again."

She replied, "I know he will rise again in the resurrection at the last day."

I said to her, "I am the resurrection and the life. He who believes in me will live, even though he dies; and whoever lives and believes in me will never die. Do you believe this?"

She said, "Yes, Lord, I believe that you are the Christ, the Son of God, who was to come into the world." [94] I asked her to get Mary for me, and she returned to the house. I waited for them. Many people had gathered at their house to offer their sorrow and to help, and when Mary ran out to come to me, they followed her.

When Mary reached me, she fell to the ground and said, "Lord, if you had been here, my brother would not have died." [95]

When I saw her, Martha, and the people who had come out with her, I was struck, for they were all weeping, and a great pressure of sorrow rose within me, ignoring my thoughts, which knew that all would be well. I said, "Where have you laid him?" [96] They began to lead me to him, but as we went, I gave way to tears, for I could not control myself.

I heard some of the people say, "See, how he loved him!" [97] But others said, "Could not he who opened the eyes of the blind man have kept this man from dying?" [98] As we approached the memorial tomb, I again felt Spirit groan within me, but I took strength. I ordered them to take away the rock that closed the mouth of the tomb, and I brought Lazarus to life. When he came out, they unwrapped him, and his skin was like that of a young man.

Many of the people who had come to console Mary and Martha were from Jerusalem, which was only a few miles away, so news of the resurrection came quickly to the Pharisees. When the high priests heard the news, they and the Pharisees summoned the Sanhedrin, the high court of the Jews, and they reasoned that the people might take faith in me as a whole. They were afraid of their positions and of the reactions of Rome, so after they conferred, they decided I should be put to death. After that time, I could no longer walk about in public, so my disciples and I fled to Ephraim, which was near the wilderness, and we stayed there.

As the Passover approached, I knew the time had come, and I could wait no longer. I gathered the twelve, and we left Ephraim, heading in a great circle north up into Galilee and then east across the Jordan into Perea and following the river south until we crossed over again, heading for Jerusalem and the final day. As we headed south toward Judea, great parties of traveling Jews joined us on the road, all heading for Jerusalem, as we were. I healed everyone who came to us with a disease: the blind, the deaf, the lepers, and the ones with twisted limbs. I spoke as we went, sometimes arguing with angry Pharisees and sometimes confiding with my disciples whatever they could hear. We passed through Jericho, and a great throng followed us out of the city up the long climb toward Jerusalem.

When we reached Bethany, there were but six days until the Passover. Martha knew we were coming, and she had arranged for a great evening meal for my disciples and me. There were to be many in attendance, so Martha had arranged to have the meal at the home of a man named Simon, who was wealthy but faithful, being a leper I had cured. It was an elaborate meal, and as was usually the case, Martha was occupied with all the things that needed to be done, while Mary sat near me, listening and watching to make sure I would need for nothing.

Early in the dinner, as we were reclining, Mary brought out a flask of oil, applied it to my feet and my head, and dried my feet with her hair, as she had done when I first met her at the house of the Pharisee in Nain. The oil was precious, worth about a year's wages, and beautiful; the intoxicating scent filled the whole room. As was often the case, Mary came under criticism for her attention to me and her lack of concern for anything else. This time, the objection came from my disciples, who were embarrassed by her extravagant gesture and said, "Why this waste?" for she seemed determined to use the entire flask, which would be almost a pound.

Judas added to the concern by saying, "Why is it this perfumed oil was not sold for three hundred denarii and given to the poor people?" [99]

I came to Mary's defense by saying, "Let her alone. Why do you try to make trouble for her? She did a fine deed toward me. For you always have the poor with you, and whenever you want to you can always do them good, but me you do not have always. She did what she could: she undertook beforehand to put perfumed oil on my body in view of the burial. Truly I say to you, wherever the good news is preached in all the world, what this woman did shall also be told as a remembrance of her." [101] After I spoke, they all let her alone.

Within a few hours, the Pharisees learned about the dinner, and they decided they would kill Lazarus as well as me, for he represented a sign that the people could not ignore.

It was early Sunday morning by the calendar of the modern world, and there were only five periods of daylight before the Passover meal that would take place Thursday night. My disciples and I left Bethany and proceeded over the Mount of Olives toward Jerusalem. It was only a few miles to Jerusalem, and as we came over the hill and looked down on Bethphage, which nestled on the eastern slope of the mountain, I sent John and Philip into the town. I told them they would come upon an ass with a young colt beside her, tied to a railing. I instructed them to untie the animals and bring them to me, and if anyone stopped them, they were to say, "The Lord needs them." [102] They said those words to the men who questioned them, and the men allowed the disciples to go on their way.

The disciples did not realize it at the time, but those things occurred so that the prophecy of Zechariah the prophet might be fulfilled, for he said, "Rejoice greatly, O Daughter of Zion! Shout, Daughter of Jerusalem! See, your king comes to you, righteous and having salvation, gentle and riding on a donkey, on a colt, the foal of a donkey." [103] But it was a sad moment for me because I knew Jerusalem would receive me with bitterness underlying the jubilation.

As I placed my outer robe on the back of the colt, the disciples spread their own on the mother, as they would not be less than their master in humility, and I rode the colt toward the city. As we grew closer, the crowds gathered in front of us, and they began to throw their outer robes onto the path before me and cut palm branches and strew them along the way. The people cried out, "Blessed is the king who comes in the name of the Lord!" and "Peace in heaven and glory in the highest!" [104]

Some of the Pharisees told me to rebuke my followers, but I said to them, "I tell you, if they keep quiet, the stones will cry out." [105]

As we drew near Jerusalem, the morning sun was full on the city, and the temple shone like a jewel. It reminded me of my first sight of the city when I was a boy, and emotion rose within me so that I could not help but cry, knowing what might have been. I reasoned to myself, yet I spoke all things out loud. "Jerusalem, if you, even you, had only known on this day what would bring you peace—but now it is hidden from your eyes." [106] Spirit rose within me so that I spoke a prophecy that was bitter to my tongue. "The days will come upon you when your enemies will build an embankment against you and encircle you and hem you in on every side. They will dash you to the ground, you and the children within your walls. They will not leave one stone on another, because you did not recognize the time of God's coming to you." [107] Just thirty seven years later, that prophecy would come about in the Romans' bloody capture of Jerusalem and destruction of the temple.

The crowd kept going before me and growing, for the people were telling others about the resurrection of Lazarus, and soon the whole city was in commotion, wanting to know "Who is this?" Seeing that, the Pharisees lamented, and they said, "Look how the whole world has gone after him." [108]

It was an hour of glory, although I knew it was on the surface only, provided to me as a gift from the Spirit. I allowed the people to rejoice, and I rejoiced with them.

That day, I went to the temple and taught, and people again brought those who had not been cured, and I made them whole. Young boys in the temple cried out, "Save, we pray, the Son of David." [109] At that, the Pharisees became incensed and cried to me, asking if I heard what they were saying, and I reminded them that it was King David who had said, "From the lips of children and infants you have ordained praise." [110]

After I had finished teaching, I looked around the entire temple, and then I called my disciples so that we might depart the city and return to Bethany.

When we reached the outer wall, I wanted to take care of something I had noticed the day before, so I walked to the tables of the money changers and vendors, once again proceeded to overturn their tables, and drove them out, saying, "Is it not written, 'My house will be called a house of prayer for all the nations?' but you have made it a den of thieves." [112] They were using the needs of the people to cheat them.

I spoke plainly that day, saying, "The hour has come for the son of man to be glorified, for I tell you truthfully, unless a grain of wheat falls to the ground and dies, it remains just one grain, but if it dies it bears fruit." [113] I talked to the people about the importance of not putting too much stock in this life and tried to explain to them that the man with pure vision was not happy with the things of this world but would be overjoyed with the things of the new one, and if he would believe in me, he would see that new world, although there would be hardship involved in following me. I became weighed down by the pressures coming in upon me, for I knew the people did not really understand my words, and I could feel the presence of the dark spirit beginning to press upon me. It knew now that I would not resist, and taking that as weakness, it began to gather in strength, becoming palpable. I continued. "Now my soul is troubled, and what shall I say? 'Father, save me out of this hour?' No, it was for this reason I came to this hour." [114] I cried out but humbly, "Father, glorify your name," [115] and I put away my concerns in submission.

As I paused to let the self-correction I had made sink in, a great voice came from above: "I both glorified It, and I will glorify It again." [116] It was the voice of God.

The people were amazed and afraid about what might happen, but I said to them, "This voice has occurred not for my sake, but for your sakes. Now there is a judging of this world, now the ruler of this world will be cast out." [117]

After that, the spirit of evil backed away from me for a time, but it went into the crowd, and they immediately said, "We heard from the law that the Christ remains forever. How is it you say that the son of man must be lifted up, who is this 'Son of Man'?" [118]

We continued teaching, but it was the same; it was as if they could not hear. At twilight, we again departed for Bethany, to the home of Martha, Mary, and Lazarus, where we were staying.

The next day we returned. I knew this was the last day I would spend at the temple. But I felt strong. I looked to the horizon and beyond so I could feel the full expanse of Spirit, and I thought about what I would say and do that day. I wondered if I had left anything out, if there was something I could do to help my disciples or anyone who might be on the verge of understanding. I could not think of anything, so I decided to limit what I said to prophecy draped in allegory, knowing it would be available to those later on who would have a better perspective on things and be able to see more clearly what had happened and why.

Before I had even arrived at the temple, the Pharisees were out to challenge me, but I answered their question with a more difficult one, and when they could not answer, I refused to answer them. Perhaps it was a small human satisfaction I allowed myself. Later, when their nagging had subsided and we were at the temple, I told a story for the benefit of my followers, to show them the Pharisees were not merely confused and well intentioned at heart but were motivated by the same selfish forces that created such pain and suffering on the earth.

The story goes like this. A certain man planted a vineyard, and he worked hard to make it good. He built a fence around it, dug a winepress, and erected a tower that would serve as a dwelling and a place of refuge. Since he was going away to a far land, he rented the vineyard out to a group of men who were to operate it and keep its produce, giving him only a small share each year. When the end of the first productive year came, the man dispatched a servant to go and see how things were going and bring some of the wine, as had been agreed. However, when the servant arrived, the tenants took hold of him and beat him, and when the man sent others, they did the same; some they stoned, and some they beat to death. Finally, the man sent his own son, thinking they would come to their senses and make amends, but the men, knowing he was the heir to the vineyard, killed him as well, hoping to make the vineyard their own.

At that point, I asked the religious leaders around me in the temple, "What, now, will the owner of the vineyard do?"

They answered easily, "Because they are evil, he will bring an evil destruction upon them and will let out the vineyard to other cultivators, who will render him the fruits when they become due." [119]

By their own words, they condemned themselves. I gave further warnings from scripture, and when the Pharisees realized I was referring to them, they surged forward to kill me, but they decided better of it, for the large crowd knew I was a prophet, and it would have been difficult to take me.

I was not yet through, so I told another illustration. I said that the kingdom of heaven had become like a king who prepared a great marriage feast for his son. The king sent his servant out to call all those who were invited, but for one reason or another, they refused to come. The king sent servants out again, and they all said, "Look, the food is prepared and the tables are set," but again, they would not come. Some went to their own fields to work, and some went to their businesses, but the rest mistreated his servants and killed many of them.

The king grew angry and sent his armies, and they destroyed the men and burned their cities. Then the king told his servants, since the feast was prepared, to go to the roads outside the city and ask anyone they met to come to the feast. When the feast was underway, the king came in to see how things were going, and when he saw a man who was not wearing a marriage garment, he asked the man how he had gotten in without a marriage garment. The man was speechless, and the king had him thrown out. "For many are called, but few are chosen," [120] I said in conclusion.

I realized that story was not for those around me listening but for the future. The first servant represented my ministry, and the second group of servants stood for the time to come when my disciples would receive my Holy Spirit after I had ascended and go out to preach to Israel for a time equal to my work—both attempts that would fail to bring Israel to the status of accepting what God had offered.

But I will tell you now that the man who is discovered without a marriage garment represents Christians throughout history and today who think they understand but do not and who, despite their sense of believing they are invited, do not have the approval of God because they do not do the things that are truly in harmony with truth and do not seek the truth with sincerity, humility, and kindness, as is required. If they had looked, they would have seen that the servants were making wedding robes available to all who came, because the king knew many of them were poor, even in spirit. What they needed would have been provided if they had asked, but because of the ease with which the invitation came, they were smug and felt their lack of respect would be of no consequence.

Even as I was saying those words, the Pharisees and the high priests, along with the officers of Herod, were trying to find a way to capture me without arousing the crowd. They sent a group of shrewd men to try to corner me with their questions so they could raise doubt in the crowd and take the opportunity to seize me. One of the questions concerned the resurrection, and they gave me an analogy that went like this: There was a man who was happily married, but he died, and his brother married his wife. In our tradition, if a man died, it was considered good if the man's brother married the widow, for he would be likely to take good care of her and raise her children with love. As it turned out, the second brother died, then the third, and so on, until the woman ended up being married to all seven brothers. They asked me, "In the resurrection which man will be the woman's husband?" [121]

I looked at them and merely shook my head, and I said to them, "Is not this why you are so stupid, not knowing either the scriptures or the Power of God? For when they rise from the dead, neither do men marry nor are women given in marriage, but are as angels in the heavens." [122]

I said that to answer them and to confuse them, but since it has confused many people from that time on, leading many to think I meant there would be no gender in the new world, I will explain some of it to you now, as it is known by the wise. When man is resurrected, it will be to the new world of God. This world will be without Satan or the influence of evil of any kind, and it will have the glory of the light of God and the Son of God and the full help of God's Spirit. When a creature is in harmony with the Spirit of God, he is led by that Spirit, just as I was when I lived upon the earth. When a man is led by Spirit, he is free, and when man is in harmony with God, there is no need of marriage or other laws that govern the actions of men, for men will know the law, and it will be in their hearts, just as it is with the angels.

"What is the greatest commandment in the law?" [123] they asked me next.

I gave them my words, which are well known on the earth but largely ignored. "Love the lord God with all your heart, and with all your soul and with all your mind, this is the first and greatest commandment, and the second is like it. Love your neighbor as yourself." [124] If we had done those things, God would not have had to create the law or send the prophets.

It was a long day, and that sort of thing went on until the late afternoon, for I continued to denounce them as hypocrites and liars, which they were, and it is the same today, for the leaders of men are liars and hypocrites, and the people are misled, just as they were.

Many of the crowd listened with pleasure but not the Pharisees, and at the end, I was distressed. I said out loud how I had wanted to bring comfort to the people, but they would not have it, so I said to all Jerusalem, "Look! Your house is abandoned to you." [125]

The disciples and I made our way out of Jerusalem for the last time. As we passed the temple, the disciples marveled at the great temple walls, which were indeed impressive: in places, each stone was higher than the height of a man, and even more in thickness and length.. I suppose after such a difficult day, even the strongest of them was shaky, and they welcomed the thought of something as solid and secure as the sight of those great stones laid, seemingly endlessly, one upon the other with design and purpose. I felt their need, but I was not going to deceive them. I knew that what they really wanted they would have to look for elsewhere, so I said to them, "Do you behold these great buildings, and these great walls, by no means will a stone be left here upon a stone and not be thrown down." [126] I know that seemed a bit oppressive to them, but it was not I who made it so.

They were quiet for a while, thinking about what I'd said and wondering what it was really all about, and I issued Spirit to them to help them contain the matter. When we came to the eastern slope of the Mount of Olives, we sat down to rest and look out over the city and the great temple. It was a beautiful place, warm with the spring. The gentle trees were bright with new growth, and the color of the new flowers gave soft diversion to the eye. I went off a little way to sit, breathe the sweet-smelling air, and relax.

A few minutes passed, and it seemed we had all regained our strength, for Peter, James, Andrew, and John came over to me; they had obviously been thinking about what I had said concerning the temple, my prophecy regarding the destruction of the temple, and my sayings that talked about the end of the world and my return to it as King, and they wanted to know specifically what I'd meant. I sensed they had accepted that I was leaving them, and they wanted that question, which remained a mystery, answered plainly before I left. John asked me directly, though they obviously had composed the question among themselves. "Tell us, when will this happen, and what will be the sign of your coming, and of the end of the world?" [127]

While I was thinking, the other disciples came over, and I began to answer the question. I told them truthfully again that no one knew the exact time of the end of the world—or the end of the present system, as we more precisely put it in our own language—but God himself. Even I could not tell them exactly what the future held, for as I mentioned before, I had not yet accomplished the most important reason for my life.

In the answers I gave to my disciples that day on the Mount of Olives, I gave my final prophesies to them. I said many things that were also meant for the people who will read this story, and I wonder that they are not better understood, at least the plain things, such as, "For nation will rise against nation and kingdom against kingdom, and there will be food shortages and earthquakes in one place after another. All these things are a beginning of pangs of distress." [128]

The earth has always had conflict and disaster, but the intractable nature and scope of the problems today should be a clue. Consider the following: "Now learn from the fig tree as an illustration on this point: Just as soon as its young branch grows tender and it puts forth leaves, you know that summer is near. Likewise also you, when you see all these things, know that he is near at the doors. Truly I say to you that this generation will by no means pass away until all these things occur." [129] These words give a finite amount of time from when these things are recognizable until their completion. "And this good news of the kingdom will be preached in all the inhabited earth for a witness to all the nations; and then the end will come." [130] This shows that we are talking about a final event.

"When the Son of man arrives in his glory, and all the angels with him, then he will sit down on his glorious throne. And all the nations will be gathered before him." [131] Are not the words angels and nations enough to show that this event concerns both heaven and earth? Further, this is repeated: "And then the sign of the Son of Man will appear in heaven, and then all the tribes of the earth will beat themselves in lamentation, and they will see the Son of man coming on the clouds of heaven with power and great glory." [132]

It was Wednesday morning. On Thursday afternoon, my disciples and I would leave our hosts and travel to Jerusalem for the Passover dinner. Until then, I wanted to do nothing. At the house of Martha, Mary, and Lazarus, I felt very much at home, even more than at Capernaum with my disciples, although I loved that place and all it had offered me. But here it was almost as if I were once again in Nazareth, before the weight of knowledge had called me from that house and that life. I dislike using the words knowledge and weight in the same breath, but it is true they come together, though it should never be a discouragement, because the strength and joy that come from truth make the weight little more than a feeling of purpose.

On that day, I wanted as little of the weight as I could manage, and my friends made it so I could scarcely keep my feet on the ground. There was no doubt Martha made me feel happy, and on that day, she made a point to be with me. For the first time since I had known her, she left the preparations to the others—I think to show me she remembered the advice I had given her some months before about being so busy looking after others that she forgot to enjoy herself.

The day went slowly, with lots of time for simple talk and a chance for some of the twelve to single me out and ask me about something that was bothering them or some concern for the future, and I was able to say to each one privately how much I cared for him and how proud I was of him. Judas was withdrawn and said little, although he did not think I knew about his intentions. After midday, he made an excuse to go, saying he had things to do regarding our belongings, but he went off to Jerusalem, and there he made an agreement with Caiaphas, who was meeting with the elders and the chief priests, to betray me. He agreed to lead them to me at a moment when I would be away from the crowds and easy to seize.

We had a beautiful meal, and Mary once again rubbed the fine hard into my feet and my hair, for she had saved a portion from the feast at Simon's house. Although I know she would have used it all that evening simply to prickle her critics, when I had defended her, she had saved enough for that night. That oil was to be the final dressing for my burial, which I had alluded to with double meaning the other night. The scent of the fine oil Mary had applied to me filled the room in such a beautiful way that I knew Spirit had augmented it, perhaps as a sign of just how wonderful things were to be one day upon the earth.

At the end of the evening, I took Martha aside and put my arms around her. As I hugged her, the pressure of her flesh seemed to melt away, and it was as if my body were falling into a void without end. There was nothing carnal about our embrace; Martha was as well versed in the law as I was, and we had both long since dealt with any spark of desire that might have arisen to tempt us, but I loved her deeply. She represented the completion of my limited relationships with women in a romantic way on the earth. I kissed her cheek, andwe retired to our rooms.

Chapter Eleven

We left for Jerusalem late the next morning, and we took our time. We stopped on the Mount of Olives, and I sent John and Peter into the city to prepare the room where we would have the Passover meal. I had arranged the place in secret because I knew Judas had betrayed me, and I did not want our last meal together to be disturbed by those who sought to capture me.

The ten and I remained on the mountain, overlooking the sunlit city and the temple. We did not speak a great deal, and when evening was approaching, we got up and made our way to the place I had arranged.

We climbed the stairs to the large upper room where we were to eat, and it was ready. With the help of our host, Peter and John had made the room everything I could have asked for. It was sparse, but the table and the furnishings were good, and the result was a comfortable and kind ambiance filled with light and a certain majesty. After we had reclined for the meal, a small silence came over us as our eyes surveyed the table and then came together over it. "I have greatly desired to eat this Passover with you before I suffer," [133] I said. With that, wine was poured, and we began to eat and drink.

After I accepted the third cup, I passed it to John, saying, "Take this and pass it from one to the other among yourselves, for I tell you, from now on I will not drink again from the product of the vine until the Kingdom of God arrives." [134]

I then rose, took off my outer garment, wrapped a towel around myself, and went about washing the feet of each man and carefully drying them with the towel. Peter refused to let me wash his feet, feeling it was improper for a man of my importance to do such a lowly thing. I reproved him, for I wanted them to know that if I was willing to serve them as their master, how much more willing should they be to serve each other? After I had given the disciples that sincere lesson regarding the importance of being humble and trying to help each other as equals, I returned to my place. Although I was still amused by Peter's reaction to my washing his feet— after I had corrected him, he'd suggested I may wash his hands and head also—I turned to another matter. I said, "He that used to feed on my bread has lifted up his heel against me." [135] In the silence that followed, I became upset, and I said frankly, "One of you will betray me." [136]

They also became troubled, and one by one, they said, "It is not I, is it?" [137]

Even Judas said it.

As I dipped my bread into the common bowl, I went on to say that it was indeed one of the twelve, and I explained that although it was true I must go away, it was a dire thing for the man who betrayed me. With that, I turned to Judas and said, "What you are doing get done more quickly." [138] The other disciples did not know what I meant by that, thinking I had asked him to do one chore or another in preparation for the rest of the festival, but at that moment, Satan took the opening in Judas' heart, and he rose and went out into the night.

When he had gone, I relaxed, and after a while, I took a loaf of bread and said a prayer of thanks over it. I then broke off a piece for each man, and I told them to eat it. I said, "This means my body which is to be given in your behalf. Keep doing this in remembrance of me." [139] When they had eaten, I took the fourth cup of wine and said a prayer over it, and as I passed it to them, I told them to drink and said, "This cup means the new covenant by virtue of my blood, which is to be poured out in your behalf." [140]

A little later, a dispute arose between Peter, John, and James as to who was the greatest among them, partly because of the wine and partly because I saw that they still had not gotten the message concerning the dangers of wanting to place one man above another. I stopped them and said to them with all seriousness that they should take a look at themselves and at the world and the plight of men. Their kings and rulers lorded it over them even with the power of death, and even the petty men with authority made their lives miserable and still wanted to be called benefactors. I pointed out that in fact, I was the greatest among them, but I'd spent my life nurturing them, and that was what ministering must mean to them: to absolutely reject the idea that any man was of more value than any other, until that judgment was finally made by God. Until then, it was their duty to try to make the other man more worthy than they. When that had sunk in, I said to them, "I make a covenant with you, just as my father has made a covenant with me, for a kingdom, that you may eat and drink at my table in the kingdom, and sit on thrones to judge the twelve tribes of Israel." [141]

After I had made that covenant with my disciples, I also gave them a command: "I give you a new commandment, that you love one another; just as I have loved you, that you also love one another." [142] At the moment I was speaking, we were all judged under the law of Moses, but as my death was to be the fulfillment of the law of Moses, after I was gone, my new commandment was to remain as the single one upon which hung the sword of justice. I spoke to them about other things that night, repeating the promise that my Father would send the Spirit to them as their helper, and I prayed to my Father in their presence, asking that he look after them. We sang songs, as was our tradition.

It was getting late, and I could see they were still troubled, so I said to them, "I leave you peace, and I give you my peace … Do not let your hearts be troubled, neither let it be afraid." [143] I explained, "If you loved me, you would rejoice that I am going my way to the Father, because the Father is greater than I am." [144]

Shortly after that, I felt the touch of blackness, and I said, "I shall not speak much with you any more, for the ruler of the world is coming. And he has no hold over me." [145] Feeling the pressure of the night close around me, I said, "Get up, let us go from here." [146]

We left the room and headed back toward Bethany. As we walked, I continued to talk. I reminded them that I would send the Spirit of God to them, and that Spirit would bring back to them all the things I had said. I mentioned that again because when I had explained to them that the ones who loved me would observe my words, for which the Father would love them, they were all straining to remember the things I had said to them over the past years and were having trouble recalling them. Now they knew what I had said to them, for the commandment to love included those things but also to bear fruit.

They had to know how to describe me and who I was according to scripture to plant the seeds in men who had no knowledge of me or who I was. The Word would become "This means everlasting life, the taking in knowledge of you, the only true God, and of the one whom you sent forth, Jesus Christ." [147] The knowledge contained in scripture allows a man the spark that will ultimately clear away the web of illusion that is over the earth, disclosing the truth.

It was after midnight and cool, but the night was oppressive. It felt thin, and quick things seemed to tear the fabric of the dark and disappear. I felt the pressure of fear trying to find a hold upon me, but I would not let it. However, some thoughts had a ring of truth, and I let them enter my mind so I could think about them. My body felt sensitive, and I felt the grasp of unfriendly hands. I knew I had to let go—I had to surrender to what lay ahead of me—but it was that itself that made it more difficult for me. If I could have called upon the Spirit to defend me or allowed it to work through me so I could defend myself, I would have found strength in the power I exerted to protect myself, and as the universe had no judgment against me for error, I would have prevailed against any force that came upon me. But I was not able to do that, for I had agreed with the will of God that I accept however the world chose to deal with my presence.

The trouble was that since I could not rally the forces of truth in my defense, I suddenly found that I was weak, and the thought was pressing that the act of allowing myself to be overcome could leave the world with the impression that perhaps I was not who I claimed to be. They might say, "After all, look at him now. Where now is all his arrogance?" Those thoughts were strong, and I was filled with an icy chill that seemed to make it even more difficult to dispel them.

We came to the garden of Gethsemane, a place on the first slope of the Mount of Olives, where the twelve and I had often come to escape the throng, talk, and pray. I was nervous, for I did not want to be captured in the state of mind I was in. I asked eight of the men to remain at the entrance to the garden, and I took John, Peter, and James into the deeper parts, where we had often sat before. I confided in them, saying, "My soul is deeply grieved, even to death,"[148] for I was almost too weak to walk. "Stay here and keep on the watch with me." [149]

After moving a little away, I dropped to the ground and began to pray. "My father, if it is possible, let this cup pass away from me."

[151] Even as I said it, I knew it was not what I wanted, and I added, "Yet not as I will, but as You will." [151]

I realized I was going to be given over to crucifixion, a fact I had never given my full attention. To be crucified was the worst of deaths in terms of shame, for such a man had no pity from his fellow man. The judgment itself testified that he had done something despicable and was receiving the rightful fate of a blasphemer. The thought pounded at me that perhaps I had done something wrong, and perhaps to die in that fashion might in some way take away from the sanctity of God's name, upon which I had relied and of which I had spoken frequently.

I continued to pray but found no answer, so I turned to John and Peter for support. I saw that they were in deep sleep. "Could you men not so much as watch one hour with me? Keep on the watch and pray continually, that you may not enter into temptation." [152] Even as I said the words, I realized that the full power of the force of darkness was upon us, and the only way their bodies and minds could survive was to become unconscious, so I said almost to myself, "The spirit, of course, is eager, but the flesh is weak." [153]

I went a farther distance away and prayed again, feeling that something must be out of order, but I could determine nothing, and again, when I returned, the three were asleep. With some resignation, I roused them, but they could say nothing.

A third time I retired to prayer, and on my knees, I asked again that this type of death not occur. To die as a man who cursed God simply did not seem right. How could that bring glory to my Father? I continued on my knees and simply let the black force be within me, doing and saying what it would as I stood aside, helpless but separate. I could feel the storm of thought rage through my body, screaming its sharpened half truths and searching for my own concession to its truth. But I was secure then, although the sheer force of the malignant spirit wracked my body and blood seeped through my skin, wrung from my body by the emotions that my nervous system could not contain.

I pulled myself up and walked back to where Peter, James, and John were again huddled in sleep. I said to them, "At such a time as this you are sleeping and taking your rest?" [154] But I said it with a note of humor, for I had regained myself. I said to them, "It is enough. The hour has come. The

Son of Man is betrayed into the hands of sinners. Get up, let us go. Look, my betrayer has drawn near." [155] I saw the lights of torches and heard the clamor of a mob.

The three and I joined the others at the entrance to the garden, and we watched as the crowd of men approached. It was a large group made up of soldiers, Pharisees, and a few common people who had followed along behind. It was dark, and I saw that the soldiers did not recognize me but were looking from one man to the next. Judas then approached me and said,

"Good day, Rabbi." [156] He kissed me on the cheek.

"Fellow, for what purpose are you present?" [157] I asked him, and then I said, "Judas, do you betray the Son of Man with a kiss?" [158] I knew the kiss was the way Judas had arranged to identify me to the soldiers. I stepped past him and into the light of the torches. "Who are you looking for?" [159] I asked. The commander of the guards said, "Jesus the Nazarene."

"I am he," [160] I said, taking another step forward. As I stepped farther into the light, Spirit brightened my image, and the men moved back, many of them falling to the ground.

"I told you I am he," [161] I said, tired of the game. "If therefore it is I you are looking for, let these go." [162] While I still had some authority, I wanted to indicate to the disciples that they need not be bound with me, and I also wanted the soldiers to be discouraged from capturing them as well. The soldiers regained their composure, came to me, and bound my wrists.

As they did so, Peter seemed to suddenly realize what was going to happen, and he called to me, "Lord, shall we strike with the sword?" [163] As was Peter's way, he acted before I could speak: taking one of the swords we had with us, he moved to the crowd and struck off the ear of a man in the front of the group of officials.

Now, some have said that Peter missed the man only to strike the ear, but that was not the case, for Peter was skilled, and he cut the man's ear off as an attempt to make the men withdraw. I did not want my men killed, so I stopped him, and I loosed the bonds around my wrists, lifted the man's ear up to his head, and healed him. After correcting Peter, I explained to my disciples, and for the sake of the Pharisees, "How would the scriptures be fulfilled that it must take place this way? [164] The cup that my father has given me, should I not drink it?" [165]

I then turned directly to the crowd and asked them, "Have you come out with swords and clubs as against a robber, to arrest me? Day after day I used to sit in the temple teaching, and yet you did not take me into custody. But all this has taken place for the scriptures of the prophets to be fulfilled." [166]

The commander of the soldiers and several of his men advanced upon me and bound me again. The disciples were pushed back, and they began to flee. In the crowd was a young man, a follower of mine named Mark. Judas recognized him, and the soldiers attempted to seize him, but he pulled out of his linen tunic and escaped.

They took me to the home of the influential former high priest Annas. Annas had been the high priest when I attended the temple as a boy, and after the allotted time, his sons also had become the high priest. At the present time, the name of the high priest was Caiaphas, who was Annas' son-in-law. Annas was a powerful man in the land of Israel. He'd ordered the soldiers to bring me to him in order that his son-in-law, Caiaphas, might have time to bring together the Sanhedrin, the holy court of the land. Annas began to question me about my teaching and my disciples, but I said, "I have spoken to the world publicly. I always taught in a synagogue and the temple, where all the Jews come together; and I spoke nothing in secret. Why do you question me? Question those who have heard what I spoke to them. See. These know what I said." [167] I indicated the Pharisees and the soldiers present.

A soldier standing near me struck me in the face, saying, "Is that the way you address the chief priest?"

"If I spoke wrongly," I replied, "bear witness concerning the wrong. But if rightly, why do you hit me?" [168] They led me away, still bound, to Caiaphas.

The Sanhedrin was composed of seventy-one men, yet the front room of the high priest Caiaphas could contain them all in comfort. Soon they were all present, but they had been delayed in finding witnesses against me. Such a trial, in the dark of the night on Passover, was not within the law, but they continued because they had already decided to put me to death. I had become composed again, and as I looked on, the room took on a sense of unreality; the harsh, cruel countenances of the men held little similarity to the image I and my people in general held of the great court.

After a long time, two witnesses were brought forward. One said, "We heard him say, 'I will throw down this temple that was made with hands and in three days I will build another not made with hands.'" [169] Caiaphas asked me, "What is it these are testifying against you?" [170]

I remained silent, and the witnesses began to squabble with each other, not able to make their stories agree. I watched Caiaphas as he walked away disappointed and then turned toward me, satisfied with his thoughts. "By the living God I put you under oath to tell us whether you are the Christ the Son of God!" [171]

Although I rarely said such a thing directly, I had no intention of lying, so I said, "I am; and you persons will see the Son of Man sitting at the right hand of power and coming with the clouds of heaven." [172]

Caiaphas, in a dramatic display, ripped his garments and exclaimed, "He has blasphemed! What further need do we have of witnesses? See! Now you have heard the blasphemy. What is your opinion?"

"He is liable to death," [173] the Sanhedrin proclaimed unanimously.

As I stood before them with my hands tied behind my back, they became bold; they jeered at me, and some struck me in the face. One priest pulled my tunic over my face, hit me with force, and called out, "Prophesy to us, you Christ. Who is it that hit you?" [174] The blows that followed seemed as little to me, and I paid attention to keeping my balance, as I did not know from what direction the next strike would come, but that soon passed, and I was taken out from the house.

I had waited for an hour or so before the dawn came, and I was taken again to another place, which I recognized as the hall of the Sanhedrin. Still clinging to some hope of respectability, the court had been called again, this time in the light of day and at the appropriate place. They started up again and asked me, "Are you, therefore, the Son of God?" [175]

I simply replied, "You yourselves are saying that I am." [176] That was enough for them, and they reasoned that they needed no witnesses, having heard it from my own mouth. With that, they led me out to the Roman governor.

As we approached the palace of the governor, whose name was Pilate, it was still early morning, and there was no one about, as it was the day after the Passover meal. I had a strange combination of thoughts and feelings. I was resigned about the injury I had received and would receive, and in some way, I was not even interested in what was happening but merely impatient that things be over with. But as we approached the steps of the mansion, I became more alert, and I oriented myself, for here I was before the great power of the world, Rome, to whom I had not even attempted to preach, and I was curious.

The men of the Sanhedrin would not enter the building, as it was considered unclean, so after a few minutes, the consul came out to us, and he stood on the steps above us and asked what we wanted of him. He was not a young man, and I thought he looked older than he was in some way, because his straight, once handsome features were somewhat puffed from the strain of office and the results of too much wine. But his eyes were intelligent and confident in the wisdom that resided in them. He was very alive and seemed to enjoy even the words that came out of his mouth, almost listening to them and reassessing them as he heard them with his own ears. I could see that he felt himself to be a part of Rome much in the way a believer felt he was a part of his own God, and when he spoke, he allowed the greater part of himself, the power and authority of Rome, to carry the words. He immediately confronted the piety of the Sanhedrin by asking them what accusation they brought against me, and he looked at me, but I could determine nothing of his assessment. The court matched his disdain and answered that if I were not a wrongdoer, they would not have brought me to him.

I knew such an approach would not succeed with this man, and he turned to go, saying, "Take him yourselves and judge him according to your own law." [177] There ensued a general uproar, and he turned back to us and waited.

A spokesman for the priests came closer and said, "It is not lawful for us to kill anyone," [178] and as Pilate hesitated, the spokesman for the group retired to the crowd and returned with a parchment. The Jews had decided not to mention their own trial, knowing Pilate might do just as he had done—instruct them to deal out their own justice, as it was a matter of religious legality. They had written down a list of charges that had at least a thread of honesty connected to their complaint with me, which they hoped would concern Rome. The spokesman read out the charges, which were three. I was charged with subverting the nation of Israel, forbidding the paying of taxes to Caesar, and calling myself Christ, a king.

I could see that at least one of the charges caught his attention, but he turned and walked away without a word. We waited for what seemed a long time, although I suppose it was only five minutes or so. The priests were uncomfortable and squirmed about, glaring at me and moving their feet, their minds busy with determination and rumination over why I was so despicable to them. Soon a guard came out and took me into the palace.

I walked up the steps and into a long marble hall carefully but thinly adorned with well-fashioned articles, including a pair of torches each twenty paces and, on each side of the corridor, a table that held ledgers with the insignias of Rome. Alcoves held busts of Caesars past and present.

At the end of the hall were three columns on each side, and passing through them, we came to a larger room, which was also marble but of a finer quality that gave off a luminescent coolness and a feeling of open grandeur. There were fine tapestries on the walls, and on the wall directly in front of me hung great banners bearing the powerful symbols of Rome. Almost in the middle of the room, facing the entrance, was a chair made of ivory and marble and adorned with little but a golden emblem, which appeared in the center of the chair's back, just above the head of the man sitting there. He watched as I approached. A table on his left—a smooth slab of marble held by carefully wrought iron—held the tools of writing.

When I was still some twenty paces from him, he told me to stop, and he looked at me. He looked to the side and then back toward me and asked,

"Are you the king of the Jews?" [179]

I wanted to know what he knew of me, so I asked him, "Is this of your own originality that you say this, or did others tell you about me?" [180]

"I am not a Jew, am I?" [181] he said with sincerity, and I knew he knew nothing of me. "Your own nation and the chief priests delivered you up to me. What have you done?" [182]

"My kingdom is no part of this world," [183] I told him slowly and deliberately. "If my kingdom were part of this world, my attendants would have fought that I should not be delivered up to the Jews. But, as it is, my kingdom is not from this source." [184]

He considered that for exactly the amount of time it would take to understand such an answer and then immediately asked, "Well, then, are you a king?" [185]

I said to him truthfully, "You yourself are saying that I am a king. For this I have been born, and for this I have come into the world, that I should bear witness to the Truth. Everyone that is on the side of the Truth listens to my voice." [186]

He paused for a moment and then said, "What is truth?" [188] Without waiting for or expecting an answer, he rose from his chair and walked past me toward the entrance, gesturing for one of the soldiers to bring me with him. When we came out, the Sanhedrin were standing as if they had not moved the whole time. He lifted his arm toward me and said, "I find no crime in this man." [188]

The Sanhedrin erupted in anger and began calling out all at once, and with a skill long perfected by the Jews, at some point, their voices became one, saying, "He stirs up the whole people, from Judea to Galilee." [189]

When Pilate heard that I was a Galilean, he knew immediately what he would do, for Herod Antipas, the ruler of Galilee, was in Jerusalem for the Passover. Pilate dispatched a soldier to Herod, and within a few minutes, I was also on my way to the ruler.

Herod was a disheveled and unpleasant man, and I immediately saw that he had no interest in me or the case against me but hoped only to see a miracle or a trick. I had nothing to say to the man, for I knew it was he who had ordered the beheading of John the Baptist, and Spirit did not urge me to talk. Herod was relieved when he saw me, for he had heard about the miracles I was doing in Galilee and had feared I was John returned from the dead with greater powers. His relief put him in a good mood, and seeing that my silence was adamant, he and his men made fun of me, but they did not harm me, and within the hour, I found myself again in the anteroom of Pilate.

Pilate called to him the Jews, who were milling around waiting for an answer. When they had gathered, Pilate said to them, "You brought this man to me as one inciting the people to revolt, and, look! I examined him in front of you but found in this man no ground for the charges you are bringing against him. In fact, neither did Herod, for he sent him back to us; and, look! Nothing deserving of death has been committed by him. I will therefore chastise him and release him." [190]

I could see that Pilate was under the impression I was an innocent man guilty only of the envy of the priests, and he wanted to release me. I was in an odd state of mind. I was not used to being dragged around from one place to another, and I too wanted it to be over. I felt little; Spirit was small within me, and I could feel no presence of the dark force. I could only wait.

So it went. The Jews would not accept my release, so Pilate proceeded with what he thought was a good idea. For the sake of the goodwill coming from such a gesture, the Romans had instituted a policy of releasing a prisoner of the Jews' choice each Passover. He called out a murderer from the prison, a man hated by the Jews, for he was guilty of many crimes against the people. He offered the Jews the choice of which one of us would be freed. As that was taking place, I began to lose interest in what was going on. I was tired, and I was having trouble concentrating. The priests spoke up loudly and incited the crowd, which had grown as the day wore on, and they all cried out, "Barabbas," for that was the name of the murderer. I began to fade into a stupor, for I could not stand to see the people so easily mislead. Among the crowd were many who had thrown palm leaves in my path as I had come into Jerusalem, and some of them I had even cured.

I was taken and flayed, and although I was numb, I stood straight when I was commanded. After I was beaten, I had little strength, but I relied on Spirit, and for the dignity of my Father, I remained tall and proud. I was taken before the people with a crown of thorns embedded in my head and a purple robe cast over my shoulders, and still, I was rejected. There was no pity among the crowd as the Pharisees continued to shout out derision and many untrue things. I looked over to see Pilate washing his hands of me, and I heard the crowd scream, "Yes, his blood upon us and our children." [191] As I looked again to Pilate, I saw in his eyes the beginning of awareness, the beginning of doubt in a world that for him had always been certain. Pilate was an astute man and fully aware of how zealous the Jews were about their piety. He had questioned me and was sure I was innocent of the charges brought against me. As a man familiar with power, he recognized it within me, and he knew my power was somehow related to matters of God, which were the exclusive domain of the priests. Yet the priests were blindly against me. On a subconscious level, that did not make sense to him. He had considered spiritual things at times, but whenever he had, he'd quickly dismissed the subject as impenetrable and a waste of time. His meeting with me had affected him, for he knew I was sincere and different from other men. He would think about it for the rest of his life.

I was taken from the palace to the place of execution.

I remember little of what happened next, except I know I opened my eyes at one point and saw John standing with my mother. I spoke to him somehow, telling him that she was his mother now, his to love and care for, and I saw in his eyes a smile, but it was soon covered by his own tears, and I looked away.

It came to be about midday, and I was fading. The little strength I had left began to slip from both my body and my mind. With the failing of my consciousness, the world began to appear dark, but I jerked awake for a moment when I noticed, with what little remaining awareness I had, a commotion in the throng. I could see from the actions and sounds of those gathered beneath me that the growing night was real to them as well. The withdrawal of my spiritual power was causing actual darkness on the face of the earth. Curiosity about that soon gave way to a deeper darkness. I was alone without light, knowledge, or time. I felt no Spirit, no sense of God, and I heard myself cry out, "My God, my God, why have you forsaken me?" [192] I knew immediately after I spoke those words that indeed, all spiritual protection had been withdrawn from me in order that I be tested to finality. Some thought I was crying out to Elijah, and they said, "See, he is calling Elijah." [193]

I felt coolness on my lips, and I instinctively drank. As the shock of the sour wine spread through my senses, it carried a great wave of warmth and light infused with a suffocating nausea. I knew it was over, and I spoke aloud in unison with the coming blackness that flowed behind the tide of sickness.

"Father, into your hands I entrust my spirit." [194] I looked out ahead of me, and the horizon lay exactly in the middle of my field of vision. A thin strip of blue ran along it, but it was dark to my eyes below the line of the earth and fading into gray and darkness above it. I closed my eyes, and I felt a great shudder as the words came from my lips and from above in one utterance: "It is finished." [195]

Chapter Twelve

The next thing I remember was opening my eyes. I saw only darkness, and as I looked into that darkness, I saw a faint quiver of light. As I focused on it, it grew into a point of brightness, and then instantly, the cave was filled with the light of a dull morning. I hesitated and then reached out within me to feel my body, and it was there. I felt a warm happiness within my stomach, and it flashed outward, filling my heart, head, arms, hands, hips, legs, and even feet. I lay silently for a moment, and then I sat up, my mind racing ahead of me, knowing it was over. I was free again. I was me!

I stood up, and behind me, with a faint brush of feeling, cotton strips wound in the shape of a body fell. My hands instinctively went to my head, and I felt a wrap of linen, which I removed and rolled into a coil. I laid it at the head of the cotton body. I glanced toward what I knew was the entrance of the cave, and as I did, the great boulder that closed the tomb silently shifted so that the light of day came in. I stood still and closed my eyes, gathering my thoughts. It was over. I couldn't quite accept the full meaning of that.

I walked to the entrance of the cave and went out. The day was shining. I looked at the trees in bloom around the garden, and they became part of me, a part of creation I was familiar with. I looked to the sky, and my vision exploded upward, faster and faster until the blue and brilliant light came to a great fullness, and the speed of my sight slowed and turned with a slow and familiar curve into the great infinity of space. Then, with a blink, I was looking at the garden once again. I looked to the horizon and saw the white squares of buildings and the hint of motion that I knew were people moving in the streets. I clenched my fists, took a breath, and then closed my eyes in happiness, for I had breath. I was alive! For a moment, I was puzzled. Did I really still have a body? I looked down upon myself, and indeed, I saw a body. I had skin and feeling. A gash still upon my side gaped open but felt whole, and I had dried blood and open wounds on both my hands and feet, but I felt no pain or concern. On the contrary, my body buzzed with energy, strength, and certainty.

Not unlike when I had come out of the wilderness fresh with enlightenment, I began to experiment just to see what I was, for human memories were flooding back into my mind. I remembered it all as the images came before me: my mother, John, John, Peter, Martha, the Pharisees, all the talk, and the closing in of darkness. I stopped there, and my mind obeyed instantly. I sank deeper into my mind and thought of God. As I did, the light of the day came within me, and I was filled with the great impulse of creation, the great brightness that held all the sound, passion, and feeling of life.

I noticed my body fading into the light, yet my human form held but without wound or wrinkle; then it gave way to a finer form still recognizable as the projection of myself but hardly to be called physical. I maintained a conscious motion toward light; my body lifted up a few inches from the ground as I caught the feeling of it. I accelerated to the point I desired, and there I was with clouds wisping by my face, their moisture tangible and pleasant. I turned to look downward toward the earth. I saw the city and the temple, which was still a jewel from any angle, and I paused for a moment to collect my thoughts. I was alive. My Father had given me life again, as had been promised. I must have succeeded! Joy punched out at me from within, and I tried to remember just what I had succeeded at. The great, broad universe of thought surrounded me, and for the first time since my awakening, I remembered it all. My heart and mind filled with the faces, names, and feelings of everything I had experienced on the earth, although the memories were confined almost entirely to the time since my baptism. I looked again to the earth. I felt an anger toward those who had grasped the world from the great, open heart of the universe and brought such anguish by convincing man through force and cunning that the earth was a small and miserable place filled by nature with pain and weakness. The anger grew, and I pulled my right arm up beside my head with my hand in a fist, as if to throw a heavy javelin of thought into the heart of the planet, but I restrained myself, and the great weight and energy my arm held relaxed back into the endless sphere of the moment. I lowered my head. No, it was not yet time.

I was alive and had a new perspective. I was drifting above the city. I lowered my head and closed my eyes in prayer. Father. There was quiet darkness under my lids. I sent up thanks and gratitude for his wisdom and help. In the peace of the depths, I began to assemble all that had happened and look ahead. I opened my eyes and saw the great turmoil of the black spirit residing in the center of the earth. I saw the serpents' heads rising up to me from the earth in their spirits, calling out to me with desperate taunts. "Are you going to kill us, Great One of God?" They called.

I met their calls without thinking. "Don't look to me for comfort, evil ones," I found myself saying. "Turn around and purify the world, and perhaps God will have pity on you." They recoiled at my words, and for the moment, I spoke no more to them.

That had broken the mood, and I moved across the sky, finding it familiar and simple. My mind was clear. For me, the end had become the beginning, but for the earth, it was not so. I was alive, and I was still a man;

I had every right to exercise my will as I chose. I was guilty of nothing, and my obligation to be passive, as had been the will of God, was gone. I heard murmuring below, and anger returned. I sent a great blast of force to the earth, commanding the demons to be silent, and I warned them that whichever one of them raised its head to me again would have to test its full strength against mine. They were quiet, and though I saw them creeping into the soil and the tiny microbes of the earth, I was content. The demons would be dealt with.

One thing stood out in my mind like a pit before the steps of sanctuary: The time of the nations must run its course. This is the time I spoke of previously, the time when the captive earth must remain burdened with the direction of Satan and the other angels who followed him to the earth, until it is evident to the great sword of universal justice that no future is possible for mankind on this present course. I thought that time must surely be close, but even as I said that to myself, I knew God would act with exactitude, at a time known only to him and according to his perfect standards. I was content with the retreat of the demons and the knowledge that it was now certain the earth would be saved. I made my way back to the surface of the planet to see the plight of my friends, plant my feet on a strong rock, and think and consult with Spirit about what was to come.

I saw a mountain peak far to the north of Judea, and I headed for it. As I lit on the top, settling onto a rock that offered a comfortable surface, I felt my body resume its human form. I was a little puzzled by that, for after taking to the air, I'd thought my human body was gone forever—at least gone from the solidity that it now took. As I looked down on my body, I noticed that my wounds were not visible, but with the simple act of my considering them, they came into view, and with a small amount of memory, I was able to make them as visceral as I wished. I settled into the side of the stone with my right shoulder, tucked my right leg up under my left thigh, and settled my left arm across my stomach, and I felt at rest. My eyes surveyed the body.

We had done a good job with this creation. The muscles and tendons of my limbs held the flesh in a smooth beauty, and the natural position of my body lent repose to the strength of bone and muscle, giving off a slight glow of power. I snapped out of my admiration of myself and pulled my body upright, summoning the mind and spirit together to think.

After I had entered into contemplation and the circle of my being stabilized to a warm, conscious light, I opened my eyes again, and I saw two white forms descending to where I sat. They were angels. I didn't recognize them by name, but as is the way with us, their names came instantly to me. I rose and greeted them. The one who was to speak said to me, "You have done well, Jesus. All things were accomplished. Would you like to see?"

I said yes, hearing my voice for the first time, and a vision filled my mind. I saw myself upon the cross and heard myself utter, "It is accomplished," in unison with a voice from heaven. That had happened, I now observed, some three hours after normal daylight had ceased upon the earth, although I remembered no such length of time. I saw that much of celestial creation had gathered in the vicinity of the earth, arranged in random harmony that extended out beyond the galaxy, with the spiritual and physical overlapping in space and time. At the moment of my death, all external light had been withdrawn from the earth. There was darkness beyond the already unnatural night that held the earth, and no light came from the temporarily isolated spirit creatures who ruled the planet.

The voice of God spoke from heaven, and the vision showed that those on the earth felt it only as a great rumble. The voice said, "The earth is free from the bonds of sin. Let every man decide to live or die without the fear of the judgment I once laid upon the sons of men. I have given the earth to my Son, and it is he who will dispense all further justice and he who rules both life and death in my name and with my Spirit." As the voice subsided, all heaven erupted in jubilation and gave praise to God for his dealings with the earth and to me for carrying out his secret plan. There was a great relief in the entire universe, for all creatures had felt the pain of the earth, and they had worried the world might simply spiral down to desolation.

I noticed in the vision that I was not present, and I remembered, of course, that at that moment, I had been without life, in emptiness with the dead of men, for the allotted time. However, they had done well without me, for the happiness extended in great brilliance and continues. The light was released again upon the earth; the world had been judged. Satan would be allowed to run his course—but at the choice and will of God—to establish once and for all the futility and inevitable harm that came from confronting the legitimacy of the Center, the Creator, to exert influence over the periphery, the creation. Satan had no further claim to man.

My death had been the single most important moment in the history of man, equal only to the moment when Adam bit the fruit. My life had allowed man the impossible: to choose life while he remained in death, choose perfection from the state of ignorance, and transcend the reality of his existence as a flawed product of a doomed action. Man was free to answer in the present the simple question that had been asked and answered in the past: "Do you wish to live as a creation of God, accepting his will?" A man would answer that question by accepting or rejecting the life I was able to offer him through the authority I now possessed as the Living Cause of the universe as it concerned the earth. I possessed that authority because I had it. I was still a man but more than a man. I was a man who was free of restriction, with the power to will whatever I chose, knowing from my heart and knowledge that my will would be in harmony with the will of my Father. I had done what I had sacrificed my prehuman life to do. I had a new existence as what I was now.

As the vision faded, I met the angel's eyes with pleasure. I saw he had something to say, so I remained quiet, and he spoke. "Officially, all this has not been sealed until you appear before your Father. But he has given you forty days upon the earth to do as you please, and then we will return to take you home." As he said those words, the angels' wings rose up and extended out at the level of their shoulders, and they began to move off and up, offering me their personal congratulations as they went. I gave myself the pleasure of lowering my head and allowing the full satisfaction of the moment to fill my being.

After a while, I myself took off, enjoying the feeling of flight without the nagging presence of the awareness that I had a body waiting somewhere to return to. I was truly myself again, whole, happy, and free.

I was still a man. That was the miracle of it all. I knew it was true that I was more than a man, but the human part of me remained intact and actual; my Father had resurrected me, not transformed me. With anticipation bursting out again, I saw that I could offer that same transformation to men now that I was free to exercise the full power of my will. Death had no permanent hold over mankind by the decree of the new judgment. I had already resurrected men in my limited life on the earth, and now those I chose to bring to life had no reason to die again. The only gloom that remained was the allotted time for the earth to fulfill its dark destiny. That thought weighed upon me, but I could only see to go ahead and do the best I could.

I returned near the tomb, where I found the entrance still open. I knew it was early morning, and I could see no one about, so I looked from above along the path to where the eleven were staying. I saw a small group of women running in that direction. I came down in front of them, allowed my body to relax into its physical form, and said to them, "Good morning," thinking that was as good as anything. I recognized Mary, the mother of James; John's mother, Salome; and Joanna, so I said to them, "Do not be afraid, but be off to the brothers, that they may go into Galilee, and there they will see me." [196]

Again, I returned to the tomb. Mary Magdalene was standing near, and angels were there. She turned and saw me, and she did not recognize me, so I said, "Mary!" She ran to me, buried her head in my chest, and put her arms around me tightly. I could feel her small, muscular frame pressing against me, and I had to smile at her intensity, but I said, "Do not hold on to me, for I have not yet returned to the Father. Go instead to my brothers and tell them, I am returning to my Father and your Father, to my God and your God." [197]

Over the next few days, I appeared several times to my disciples, and they were ecstatic that things were as they were. It was evident that despite all the times I had told them what was to happen, they really had not expected it to be so.

I did many things over the forty days—some for my own pleasure and many to solidify the faith and knowledge of the brothers. I went to my mother, and she was at peace at last. I also went to my own brothers for the sake of my mother, so they might believe. Of the other times I came to men, it is written about me. When I saw Peter, he was the most delighted of them all. I asked him three times if he loved me, and I told him each time he answered me to feed my sheep. I did so because Peter was in great pain about having denied me three times on the night of my capture. He did not understand at the time, but later, when he began to worry about it again, Spirit reminded him of my three requests to declare his love for me and explained that the three affirmations were for him to know he was forgiven and not in debt.

The last time I saw the eleven was near the Mount of Olives. I explained to them that the time of restoring the Kingdom of God to the earth was not up to us but up to God, and then, after again promising them I would send the Holy Spirit to help them, I felt a gentle tug. Responding, I drifted higher into the air. As I looked down, I saw the two angels who had come to me on the mountain speaking to the men, and then the disciples passed from my view as the clouds closed around me. I looked up toward the heavens, and as I began to move more quickly, the blue of the sky gave way to the deep black of space, highlighted by the great jewels and brilliant glowing clouds of the active creation. I was enjoying the sight, when the two angels appeared beside me and said to me, "We have been sent to bring you to your Father." With that, our travel changed to light and then to the great speed of the higher creatures of God —beyond time and space—so that I saw only the flicker of great celestial worlds, with the gentle music they made blending into a fine hum as we moved across the universe.

The throne of God changes in appearance according to his will, although it is eternally in place even when the presence of God does not sit upon the throne. Whether God is there or not, thousands of spiritual creatures are always around the throne, either doing the will of God or simply congregating and engaging the others who are there. The sacred area around the throne extends for a distance equal to all the universe perceived by man, yet such are the properties of the place that a spirit creature can see beyond the perimeter of the sacred area and view the great stars and celestial worlds that lie closest to the throne and past into the fading infinity of populated space beyond.

I had no actual memories of the Throne of God, as I had no memories of my heavenly life at all. What I knew was shown to me after my Enlightenment. The Power and the Glory of what I was in the midst of was beyond all description. It was filled with brilliance and power, heavy as a river of cool liquid gold, yet a core of serenity and peace was at the center. With it came a feeling of joy and what I can only describe as an ever expanding happiness and peace. As we entered the area, a great white pathway appeared in front of us. It became a hallway of light, translucent, with an arched roof so that we actually entered into it. I somehow knew the corridor was the welcome that accompanied a formal entry into the Court of the Living God.

When we arrived at the end of the corridor, we passed through a highly ornate arch that opened onto the inner court of the High God. On the level we were on, massive columns extended around the entire circle of the inner court. The columns surrounded a circumference so vast that on the opposite side of the throne, which appeared to be in the center of the space, they seemed as only a thin strip of gold light. I brought my attention away from being overwhelmed (and curious) about the wonderful nature of the place I found myself in.

The important part was that I was to appear before God. I cannot describe much more to you because it would begin to seem merely silly, but I hope that every man one day is able to come before God. It was a formal ceremony, as I said, and as I knelt before God, he gave me praise for the work I had done. Although what I had done seemed as nothing while I knelt before him, he denied that to the millions who watched, and He named me His Firstborn Son. I sat down at his right hand on a great throne. A crown of golden stars was placed upon my head, and I was called the King of Heaven and Earth in his name. All the creatures of heaven acknowledged this with a bow and an instant of submission, focusing, for a moment, all the power, glory, and love of the universe into the center of my being. Only certain ones were not present, for Satan would not appear.

In the heavens, we do not lord it over one another, and it was unlikely I would be called upon in my capacity as the King of Heaven for a long time by the measure of time, for all the creatures of heaven obey the will of God and the promptings of the Spirit. I had before known prominence in the heavenly worlds, being called the Word, but the honor of sitting at the right hand of God is, of course, indescribable, an infinite brightness upon an infinite brightness, and humbling.

After the acknowledgment of the court, a great angel of God came before me and handed me the scepter that went with my station, and he gave me formal authority over the earth, as had been explained to me before I ascended. He gave me the word from the Living God, my Father, that the twelve would be multiplied by their own number and then by a thousand as God's gift to me in men, so they might be given the immortality of spiritual life and reign with me over the earth for the thousand years allotted to returning the earth to perfection.

I was excused, for Spirit knew I had things to do according to the brief years of man and acts I wanted to accomplish before I rested. In that instant, a four-winged angel, a messenger of speed, approached me and took my hand, and we were again at the gates of the throne and then in the vicinity of the earth. I saw through Spirit that the eleven were gathered together in an upper room with many others. I ordered my Spirit to go to them and fill them with power beyond a man, and it did so. With that, the disciples began to teach with the authority to baptize in spirit.

My presence was upon the earth, and it is. The boundaries between the fallen earth and heaven are dissolved where they overlap with my conscious will, although this freedom is difficult for most men to avail themselves of, as it exists only in the higher attributes of man until the final day brings such truth to the physical world. My heart aches for the unbearable suffering and cruelty that exist upon the earth. I am anxious to come to you. Simply by your asking, I will offer an awareness of my presence. By faith, this will become stronger. By patience, it will be revealed. Nothing is held back by God. The only obstacle between us lies within yourself. That obstacle is formidable. Do not be distracted by the details of faith. Men make division by arguing over words and interpretations, separating church from church for their own sake. All who believe in me belong to one faith. The distance between true life and the life of man has become almost impassable. Almost nothing man thinks is true. Even the best of choices lead nowhere. But I can be reached in spirit—first by thought and intent and then by spirit. I will make myself known to you. Now.

I will not mislead you by saying this is easy. The truth is that your own self is so enmeshed in a reality created by thousands of years of incorrect thought that by the time of adulthood, it is pretty well impossible for a human to expect any clarity when it comes to Reality. The amount of love, understanding, and heroic mercy that has emerged is a great testament to the soul of man. If you are sincere—and it might take some time to get there—I will lead you through your life. I will love you as much as you allow.

Allow the Spirit to show you what things in you are deflecting the ever-present illumination of God. Do not fall prey to guilt, for through my life, you are forgiven. There is no formula other than faith. You may believe in yourself as strongly as you can and strive as hard as you can, but be honest, and do not judge yourself according to the success of this world, for there is none. If you are young, go ahead and reach for your dreams, for that comes from your divine nature. But do not be deceived: your divine nature has not yet been realized, and if you see the path to truth open up before you, take it. Ask for me, and I will come. Ask for me again, and I will come. The love of God is returning to the earth and to you.

Notes

[1] John 4:8.
[2] Matt. 3:14.
[3] Matt. 3:15.
[4] Matt. 3:17.
[5] John 1:29–30.
[6] John 1:36.
[7] John 1:38.
[8] John 1:39.
[9] John 1:42.
[10] John 1:47.
[11] John 1:48.
[12] John 1:49.
[13] John 1:51.
[14] John 2:16.
[15] John 2:18.
[16] John 2:19.
[17] Exod. 12:26–27.
[18] John 2:23.
[19] John 4:9.
[20] John 4:10.
[21] John 4:11–12.
[22] John 4:14.
[23] John 4:15–16.
[24] John 4:18.
[25] John 4:19.
[26] John 4:20.
[27] John 4:23–24.
[28] John 4:25–26.
[29] John 4:50.
[30] Luke 4:21.
[31] Luke 4:22.
[32] Mark 1:24.
[33] Mark 1:25.
[34] Mark 3:11.
[35] Matt. 9:9.
[36] Matt. 9:14.
[37] Matt. 9:15.
[38] Matt. 9:16–17.
[39] Matt. 12:2.
[40] Matt. 12:10.

[41] Matt. 12:11.
[42] Matt. 12:12.
[43] Matt. 12:13.
[44] Matt. 3:2.
[45] Luke 7:14.
[46] Luke 7:19.
[47] Gen. 3:4.
[48] Gen. 3:5.
[49] Luke 7:40.
[50] Luke 7:41–43.
[51] Luke 7:44–47.
[52] Luke 7:48.
[53] Luke 7:50.
[54] Matt. 14:28.
[55] John 6:28–29.
[56] John 6:34.
[57] John 6:42.
[58] John 6:51.
[59] John 6:53.
[60] John 6:60.
[61] John 6:67.
[62] John 6:68–69.
[63] John 5:20–21.
[64] Luke 12:51–53.
[65] Matt. 17:5.
[66] Mark 9:19.
[67] Mark 9:24.
[68] Matt. 17:22–23.
[69] John 7:4.
[70] John 7:11.
[71] John 7:24.
[72] John 7:31.
[73] John 9:16.
[74] John 9:17.
[75] John 9:25.
[76] John 9:27.
[77] John 9:28–29.
[78] John 9:30–34.
[79] John 9:35.
[80] John 9:36.
[81] John 9:36.
[82] John 9:37.
[83] John 9:38.
[84] John 9:39.
[85] John 9:40.
[86] John 9:41.
[87] Luke 10:17.
[88] Luke 10:23–24.
[89] Luke 10:21.
[90] John 11:7.
[91] John 11:8.
[92] John 11:14.
[93] John 11:16.
[94] John 11:21–27.
[95] John 11:32.
[96] John 11:34.
[97] John 11:36.
[98] John 11:37.
[99] John 12:5.
[100] Mark 14:6–8.
[101] Mark 6:9.
[102] Matt. 21:3.
[103] Zech. 9:9.
[104] Luke 19:38.
[105] Luke 19:40.
[106] Luke 19:42.
[107] Luke 19:43–44.
[108] John 12:19.
[109] Matt. 21:15.
[110] Ps. 8:2.
[111] Mark 11:14.
[112] Mark 11:17.

[113] John 12:23–24.
[114] John 12:27.
[115] John 12:28.
[116] John 12:28.
[117] John 12:30–31.
[118] John 12:34.
[119] Matt. 21:41.
[120] Matt. 22:14.
[121] Matt. 22:28.
[122] Mark 12:24–25.
[123] Matt. 22:36.
[124] Matt. 22:37–39.
[125] Matt. 23:38.
[126] Matt. 24:2.
[127] Matt. 24:3.
[128] Matt. 24:7.
[129] Matt. 24:32–34.
[130] Matt. 24:14.
[131] Matt 25:31–32.
[132] Matt. 24:30.
[133] Luke 22:15.
[134] Luke 22:17.
[135] John 13:18.
[136] John 13:21.
[137] Matt. 26:25.
[138] John 13:27.
[139] Luke 22:19.
[140] Luke 22:20.
[141] Isa. 45:18.
[142] John 13:34.
[143] John 14:27.
[144] John 14:28.
[145] John 14:30.
[146] John 14:31.
[147] John 17:3.
[148] Matt. 26:38.
[149] Matt. 26:38.
[150] Matt. 26:39.
[151] Matt. 26:39.
[152] Matt. 26:40–41.
[153] Matt. 26:41.
[154] Matt. 26:45.
[155] Matt. 26:45–46.
[156] Matt. 26:49.
[157] Matt. 26:50.
[158] Luke 22:48.
[159] John 18:4.
[160] John 18:5.
[161] John 18:8.
[162] John 18:8.
[163] Luke 22:49.
[164] Matt. 26:54.
[165] John 18:11.
[166] Matt. 26:55–56.
[167] John 18:20–21.
[168] John 18:22–23.
[169] Mark 14:58.
[170] Mark 14:60.
[171] Matt. 26:63.
[172] Mark 14:62.
[173] Matt. 26:65–66.
[174] Matt. 26:68.
[175] Luke 22:70.
[176] Luke 22:70.
[177] John 18:31.
[178] John 18:31.
[179] John 18:33.
[180] John 18:34.
[181] John 18:35.
[182] John 18:35.
[183] John 18:36.
[184] John 18:36.

[185] John 18:37.

[186] John 18:37.

[187] John 18:38.

[188] Luke 22:4.

[189] Luke 22:5.

[190] Luke 23:14–16.

[191] Matt. 27:25.

[192] Matt. 27:46.

[193] Mark 15:35.

[194] Luke 23:46.

[195] John 19:30.

[196] Matt. 28:10.

[197] John 20:17.

CPSIA information can be obtained
at www.ICGtesting.com
Printed in the USA
LVHW030725060423
743648LV00001B/24

9 781685 472115